AYŞE KULİN

After graduating from the American College (ACG) of Istanbul, Ayşe Kulin worked many years as editor and writer for newspapers and magazines and also in the cinema industry.

Her first story book won two prestigious literary awards (Haldun Taner & Sait Faik) and her first novel became a best seller. Kulin also holds other literary awards and has been selected the author of the year numerous times. Some of her stories and novels became TV series and motion pictures. Her works have been translated into German, French, Italian, Dutch, Greek, Spanish, Polish, Hungarian, Georgian, Latvian, Porrtuguese and Serbian. She is the Goodwill Ambassador of UNICEF since 2007. Her major novels translated so far:

Face to Face
Farewell

Books in Turkish

1. *Güneşe Dön Yüzünü*
2. *Bir Tatlı Huzur*
3. *Foto Sabah Resimleri*
4. *Adı: Aylin*
5. *Geniş Zamanlar*
6. *Sevdalinka* (Love Sonsg of Bosnia)
7. *Füreya*
8. *Köprü*
9. *İçimde Kızıl Bir Gül Gibi*
10. *Babama*
11. *Nefes Nefese*
12. *Kardelenler*
13. *Gece Sesleri*
14. *Bir Gün*
15. *Bir Varmış Bir Yokmuş*
16. *Veda*
17. *Sit Nene'nin Masalları*
18. *Umut*
19. *Taş Duvar Açık Pencere*
20. *Türkan-Tek ve Tek Başına*
21. *Veda* (Graphic Novel)
22. *Hayat-Dürbünümde Kırk Sene*
23. *Hüzün-Dürbünümde Kırk Sene*
24. *Gizli Anların Yolcusu*
25. *Saklı Şiirler*
26. *Sessiz Öyküler*
27. *Bora'nın Kitabı*

Ayşe Kulin

FACE TO FACE

Translated by John W. Baker

§

Puclication No **602**
Fiction **4**

Face to Face
Ayşe Kulin

The Original Title: Bir Gün
Translated by John W. Baker

Cover Design: Utku Lomlu
Page Layout by Hülya Fırat

1. English Edition: August 2008
2. English Edition: October 2009
3. English Edition: December 2011
4. English Edition: September 2014

ISBN: 978 - 975 - 289 - 531 - 7
Certificate No: 10905

Printed by: Melisa Matbaacılık
Certificate No: 12088
Tel: (0212) 674 97 23 Faks: (0212) 674 97 29

EVEREST YAYINLARI
Ticarethane Sokak No: 15 Cağaloğlu/İSTANBUL
Tel: (212) 513 34 20-21 Faks: (212) 512 33 76
e-posta: info@everestyayinlari.com
www.everestyayinlari.com
www.twitter.com/everestkitap
facebook.com/everestyayinlari

The master craved for the love of the sage
The sage for the love of master craved
Quite different were their ways
Yet for wholeness and unity they prayed.

Mevlana

TURKISH SAYINGS

Ağa	: landlord, tribe chief, influential village person.
Ana	: mother
Ayran	: a drink made of yoghurt
Bayram	: religious holiday
Bey	: Mr.
Dede	: grandfather
Dolma	: vegetable, fowl, lamb, mussel, etc. filled with stuffing / dressing.
Efendi	: sir, lord, master
Hanım	: Miss, Mrs.
Kaymakam	: official charged with governing a provincial district.
Kızılbaş	: who is member of an order of Shiite.
Kuma	: unwedded second, third, fourth wife.
Muhtar	: the elected head of a village or of a neighbourhood within a town or city.
Selamlık	: part of the house where only male guests are accepted.
Vallahi Billahi	: Islamic swear

PRONUNCIATION GUIDE

a as in father
c as in jam
ç as in chicken
e as in bed
ğ (soft g) elongates the vowel preceding it
ı as in nation
i as in piano
j as in the French "j" or the "z" in "azure"
o as in more
ö as eu in the French fleur
r somewhere between the English and the Spanish r (right and pero)
ş as in ship
u as in cool

FACE TO FACE

NEVRA TUNA – ZELİHA BORA

It is quite hot in the car but it seems as if the cold, dry air outside has gone right through my body and chilled me to the marrow. My hands and feet are frozen. I am sitting upright looking at the road ahead but nothing that I see registers, I am motionless. Both of us are as tight as bow-strings. We are travelling in silence. He is the first one to break that silence:

"We're almost there; you'd better start getting ready."

I cover my head with a large black shawl and pull the front down to my eye-brows, and then I pinch the two sides and join them tightly under my nose fastening them together with a safety pin. Hasan Bey starts laughing:

"Pull it back a bit so that at least you can see."

I awkwardly push it up a bit.

"Yeah, that's it. That's better. It suits you if I may say so; it highlights your beautiful eyes."

"I can't imagine anyone looking good in this outfit."

"You're wrong. It certainly suits women with beautiful eyes even if they have ugly noses."

"That's some compliment, thank you."

"Don't fish for compliments. You know as well as I do that you haven't got an ugly nose."

I'm getting annoyed but I can't be bothered to argue with a man old enough to be my father, especially as he is trying to help me, so I keep silent. It's very early in the morning and the dense mist is only just beginning to lift here and there. I wipe the condensation from my side window with the edge of my shawl as we continue driving ahead.

"I'm suffocating, I can't breath."

"Why not? You haven't covered your nose have you?"

"All the same I feel as if I am being stifled. Maybe it's psychological. Would you mind opening the window to let in some fresh air?"

He presses the button and lowers the window half way down. The morning frost makes us both shiver.

"Shall we go through the whole thing one more time?" Hasan Bey asks.

"OK. I'll ask all of my questions as quickly as possible without diverting from the subject. I'll make brief notes and those that I can't write down I'll keep in my head and make sure to jot them down as soon as I can. If we feel peckish we'll have the biscuits I have with me. The interview must finish by five. If there are any problems I shouldn't tackle them but call you on my mobile."

"I'm sorry to have to tell you that they won't allow mobile phones."

"What if I have a problem?"

"If there is you should ask to see Dilaver Bey."

"And who's he?"

"He's an old friend of mine. He'll be there. I'll leave you in his care."

"Can he be trusted?"

"Of course."

"Fine then."

"You seem to have forgotten the most important thing young lady."

"Rest assured I haven't forgotten anything. No one is to know about this meeting except you and... what was his name? Dilaver Bey."

"Well done."

"Hasan Bey, I shall never forget this. Really... I just can't thank you enough."

"Just pray to God, we don't get into any trouble."

"How could we? Nobody knows about it... apart from us."

"Even walls have ears," he said anxiously. "If anyone should get to hear of this, the prison governor will be in trouble."

"No one will know," I assured him, hoping that I didn't show the anxiety in my voice. "Trust me this job will be finished today. It will be over and done with without anyone knowing about it."

"*Inshallah.*"

"The tape recorder..."

"You'd better give it to me. It mustn't be found on you. I'll try and sort something out for you."

"It's in that small bag on the back seat... What a shame I can't have it, writing notes wastes time and it's not easy remembering everything."

"Thank your lucky stars for what we have got."

"Of course I do! I really appreciate what you have done for me... I can't thank you enough..." I must have thanked him a hundred times already and it was becoming a bit monotonous so I decided not to continue.

Hasan Bey turns right at the next cross-roads. We continue on our journey in silence for quite a while. We are both buried in our thoughts. Then we swerve to the left and a short while later the concrete prison wall with barbed wire on the top looms up before us. I feel as though I am gasping for air. I reach out for my bag, put it on my lap and rummage through it. I hate such deep bags they're like bottomless pits; you can never find what you're looking for in them especially when you're in a hurry. I fumble through the contents until I find my asthma medicine. I grab the inhaler and hold it tightly in my hand.

"What's up?" asks Hasan Bey.

"It must be the excitement. I feel as though I lack of breathe."

"I didn't know that you suffer from asthma. Is it an allergy? Are you sensitive to the dust in the air?"

"No, it's not the dust. The humidity affects me."

"But there's no humidity in the car... You look a bit nervous. Do you want to change your mind?"

"Absolutely not!"

The car slows down and then stops in front of an iron gate. Hasan Bey gets out and walks towards the gate. I quickly take a couple of puffs from my inhaler before he returns.

"Get out and wait for me here," he says, "I'll park the car and come back."

I get out of the car and wait on the pavement. I'm standing motionless like a statue. The black shawl on my head covers me to the waist and I'm wearing a long grey coat down to my ankles. What a frightening feeling this is, it's like being imprisoned in a tower. How can one accept being caged in such clothes of their own free will? How can the women of my religion be so passive? I slowly take a step forward... then one more, and another. At least I can walk... I walk faster and faster... twenty steps to and fro along the prison wall wearing this strange new outfit. The guard standing in front of the gate is watching me with astonishment. Hasan Bey, who has parked the car and returned, must have informed someone on his mobile phone of our arrival because a man wearing a dark blue suit comes out of the iron gate to meet us. I have never completely understood why all clerks in dark blue suits look alike. Neither have I ever been able to understand why religious merchants with long beards or MPs with bushy moustaches, all look alike. This frail and pale faced man appears to be fed up with life, possibly because he is one of the subordinates who earns a low salary. He is showing a piece of paper to the guards at the checkpoint next to the iron gate with a sad expression on his face. The guard sticks his hand through his small window and asks for our identity cards and then hands us collar badges. The other guard waiting outside opens the gate nonchalantly and we go inside. There is a large courtyard with no trees at all. There are no people either. A totally empty, open space. I am looking around me, bemused. Hasan Bey pulls me by the arm.

"Let's go young lady."

When we are away from the guards Hasan Bey leans over and whispers something in the man's ear. The man in the dark blue suit just nods his head and says nothing. We walk quickly to the building opposite and enter it. There is a control point like those at an airport, right in front of us.

"Get the palm of your hand scanned," snaps the officer.

When I look puzzled the man in the dark blue suit takes my hand and places it on the magnetic pad on the wall. Hasan Bey does the same after me.

"Since this gadget can read the palm of your hand it might as well tell your fortune too," I say but nobody smiles. Even Hasan Bey pretends not to have heard me. It seems that everybody here has to be serious and gloomy all the time! I put my bag on the conveyor belt before passing through the checkpoint.

Someone tells me sharply, "Take off your shoes!"

Both Hasan Bey and I take off our shoes and pass through the checkpoint me in my stockinged feet, he in his socks. One of the officials picks up my shoes and examines them inside and out then he hands them back to me. When I pick up my bag from the conveyor belt another official asks for my mobile phone. I take it out of my bag and give it to him.

"I'll hang on to this; you can collect it on your way out."

A plump uniformed woman points to a partition indicating that I should step behind it. She says that I should remove both the shawl and the long coat and put them on the chair in the corner. Then she walks around me and with her stubby fingers examines my body even feeling between my legs. She then says,

"You can get dressed now." As I tie the shawl around my head again I am thinking that she hasn't recognised me. I chuckle when I realise the importance I have attributed to myself. Why should she recognize me? There's only a tiny old passport photograph at the head of my column in the newspaper. I had given that old photograph to the newspaper because I looked much younger than any of the recent ones. Even if I did look like my picture just how many people would read such a repulsive left-wing paper as Sentez (Synthesis) whose columnists are all smart-arses? How silly we were to even think that it was necessary for me to adopt such a ridiculous disguise. Why did I do it? Why did I listen to Hasan Bey? But then I was willing to do anything to get this interview, that's why! Anything, just as long as he could swing this interview for me. I would be the first journalist to get in to interview this political prisoner, no one else had managed to get anywhere near her. I wanted to tear out whatever was in her heart and head. I wanted to examine every corner of her life, her loves, hopes and fears. To expose every minute detail that has brought her to this prison. And then to entrust this to paper as the most important and meaningful article of my life. For some reason best known to me I feel that I am the only person who could accomplish this mission.

I was so sure of myself. Apart from achieving something very difficult I hoped that with this article I would at last be recognised as an important journalist in Turkey.

The man in the dark blue suit leads us through another door and along a corridor; he opens a door to the right and we enter into what seems like a waiting room. We sit down on plastic chairs.

"Everything is going well, don't worry," says Hasan Bey, trying to conceal the slight anxiety he is feeling. "Dilaver Bey won't stay with you during the interview. You'll have to do it alone. That's OK isn't it?"

"OK, of course it is!" I'm trying not to show the smile on my face. It hadn't even occurred to me there might be someone else present during the interview. My God, that was a close shave, and to think it hadn't even crossed my mind. What would I have done if a third person intruded into my world designed for two, or if Hasan Bey were to say, "I'm going to sit in during the interview?" That would have spoiled any spark that I may be able to create between us for sure.

"Don't worry at all Hasan Bey. It's much better this way." When I see that he realises that I am pleased with this situation I add, "It will be more intimate this way, just woman to woman."

Another man enters the room and shakes Hasan Bey's hand. After they finish exchanging niceties Hasan Bey gets up and puts his hand on my shoulder.

"I'm afraid I have to go now but I'll leave you in the capable hands of Dilaver Bey," he says. The tall, thin, sad faced Dilaver Bey, who in his grey suit looks like a melancholic rain-cloud, takes me into his charge. "That's that then young lady, good luck," says Hasan Bey. "Ah, one more thing, I've managed to sort out the tape-recorder business... They'll bring you one. I'll come and pick you up at five o'clock. I'll be waiting at the gate. If you finish earlier just give me a call."

As I walk through the door with my new escort, Hasan Bey winks at me to signal that everything is going to be alright. Then I'm left standing alone in a small prison room. I shudder. Thank God, my loneliness doesn't last long. Dilaver Bey returns a short while later and asks me to follow him.

I walk along the stone corridor as fast as the long coat wrapping itself around my legs will allow, all I can hear are my footsteps and my heart-beat. I'm scared now. I've gone into this without considering the consequences and totally ignoring the advice of friends and colleagues. I am rather apprehensive right now. My legs are wobbly and I am sweating under this thick coat. Dilaver Bey and I are walking, walking, walking along this seemingly endless corridor. Will this journey ever come to an end? A sad song about losing ones way, sung by a favourite singer of mine, echoes in my ears. We walk up a flight of worn stone steps to the next floor. And then along another long corridor lit by a lamp. Dilaver Bey suddenly stops, takes a large key out of his pocket and opens a door on our left.

"Here we are, you can wait here," he says as he shows me in.

I go through the opened door. There are a lot of things I want to ask but Hasan Bey had warned me to say as little as possible, in fact not to say anything at all so I'm holding back my questions.

"No one will disturb you here," says Dilaver Bey. He takes my small tape recorder out of his pocket and puts it on the table. "You'd better put this in your bag for the time being. You can use it later when you need to."

"Fine," I say and immediately put it in my bag.

Dilaver Bey leaves the room and shuts the door behind him. I'm hoping that he hasn't locked me in. I want to get up and check but change my mind in case he has in fact locked the door, then how would I feel?

The room I am in is sparsely furnished. Just a wooden table in the centre with four chairs around it, lit by a yellow light from a bare light bulb hanging from the ceiling. I pull the shawl from my head, ruffle my hair and take off the long coat. Wow! What a lovely feeling it is to look like my real self again in my roll-necked sweater and skirt. My fear subsides. I remove my note-book and pencils together with the cigarettes I had put in a plastic bag and put them on the table before cramming the black shawl into my bag. I sit on a chair with my back to the door. I am waiting.

It's a long wait. Every second seems like an hour. Time is not passing. There is not a sound in the room. The silence is unbearable. Life is flowing in the outside world but here in this dreary room there is no life, only stagnant time. There is no sound of wind, rain or traffic, nothing except the sound of my own breathing. The room is windowless so there aren't even the birds to watch flapping their wings on the window ledge. Either there is no one walking along the corridor or maybe the room is soundproof. It feels as if I am being punished with an endless and treacherous silence for ignoring the rules and daring to come here. I can understand exactly how it feels to be a prisoner, holed up in a place where life stands still, time does not pass and colours don't exist. Sitting here it is hard to believe just how important those maddening noises in the real world are. A screaming child, doors slamming, loud radios and street vendors crying their wares, impatient drivers tooting their horns, the rumble of the washing machine, a dripping tap and my cleaner telling me about last night's dream or her mother-in-law's back pains... I find it strange that time does not pass without the background sounds of every-day life. This place seems to be two-dimensional; I am suffocating in this timeless atmosphere.

I hear footsteps outside; I turn to the door, prick up my ears like a dog and listen. Someone opens the door, peeps inside and then closes it again without saying a word. I can relax a bit; the door isn't locked after all. The footsteps fade away and that persistent silence returns to the room. Not a single sound. No colour, no movement. I am sitting motionless on my chair in my beige clothes. It is as though I am not real just a still sepia photograph. Suddenly my stomach's gurgling echoes like thunder in my ears. Ohh! Thank God, I am alive! That's a relief. I put my hand on my chest and listen intently to my heartbeat. I wonder if I could hear the blood flowing through my veins if I concentrated hard enough. I hadn't realised before how difficult it is to be locked up completely alone in a silent world. I ask myself if maybe, in spite of all the precautions we took, I have been found out and am now a prisoner within these stone walls myself. Will this wait never end? I gaze at the door and wonder, maybe it can be opened from the outside but not from the inside. I start to panic yet again. I leap up and start fiddling with the door-handle. The door opens. I stupidly poke my head out but fortunately the corridor is totally empty. I close the door, go back to my chair and sit down. Obviously I am not a prisoner otherwise the door wouldn't have been left unlocked, yet I am still slightly scared.

I close my eyes and breathe deeply, in and out, in and out while praying silently, "Dear God, please help me." I say this because I know that this is the last opportunity to save my job. If this interview doesn't materialise I may well be out of work. This might be my last chance to keep my newspaper column on page 5. There are many blonde young women straight off the cat-walk or straight out of the TV screen waiting to grab my column. It's a shame that when I was a long-legged dolly bird myself, newspaper columns were only written by experts and mainly by men. They had powerful pens and never moved to another newspaper. The only opportunity came when one of these dinosaurs died. Fate would have it that by the time I began loosing my dolly bird image and became an expert on interviews, the papers started hiring these bright young girls. This is why I must achieve the impossible and get this interview in order to secure my position. Months of struggling and fighting have gone into this already. I have risked everything and pulled all the strings I knew how to. I have done my best to develop a close friendship with Hasan Bey who happens to be the brother-in-law of the prison governor and also a retired police commissioner. I have been well aware that it was vital for me to come up with something really special. Was that what it's all about then? No, there is another reason for me being here and that has got nothing to do with work.

What if she changes her mind?.. What if she won't see me? Ice-cold perspiration is pouring down my back... No, no, she will come! She will come! She will come and this interview will be a turning point for me. I will shine like a star. Everyone will be talking about this interview. Most probably I will be the recipient of the Journalist of the Year award. It is even possible that this may pave the way to greater things. My bad luck needs to change one way or another. I mustn't go home, look in the mirror and say to myself, "Nevra, you've done it again, another flop on your hands." I am tired of failure, I am tired of losing. I am the idiot who destroyed her marriage with her own bare hands. I was to blame for first of all losing my husband, then my well paid job and finally my son. I am a clumsy person who never manages to complete anything. Not only did I screw up my marriage but on top of that I couldn't even keep a lover. If I fall flat on my face again today it won't be for the want of trying but I might have to return to my 7th floor office overlooking the motorway and hideous high-rise buildings, unplug my laptop, collect the few belongings from my desk, reflect on 'The reality of Turkey today' and simply walk out. But then, won't I be cutting the only thread that binds me to life? What else have I got to cling to? Exactly what? Please God let this woman, who is a saint or a sinner in different people's eyes, come and talk to me. Let this peasant girl who, in the light of recent events, has been turned into an icon; give me the chance to change my destiny.

Why isn't she coming? Why is she so late? What right does she have to steal my time when every second is as precious as gold or diamonds?

Having complained that time was standing still it now seems that it is passing with such a speed that it is mocking me. Now I'm trying to stop the passing of time with all my strength. I am scared that I will not have enough time for all my questions. So what? I'll just have to do what I can. I shall have to do my best to buy time because there is no way that I can come back to continue the interview. As long as she comes! She must come. Where the hell is she! Suddenly, as I am pacing around the table going over my questions in an effort to relieve my anxiety another thing occurs to me. What if she does come and I can't conduct the interview the way I'd like to? What if she snaps at me? Alternatively, even worse, what if I lose my temper and I end up saying, "Fine, have it your own way Zeliha Bora, that's enough!" Even if that would be going against everything I had planned, I know that I am capable of biting off my nose to spite my face... Believe me that wouldn't be something new either. I have been guilty of that too, many times in the past. Once I blow my top my ears don't hear what I'm saying!

"Aahh!" I am taken by surprise, as the door opens I jump out of my chair. Zeliha Bora is standing in the doorway with Dilaver Bey behind her. She looks tired but dignified. She has reddish brown hair cut in a bob and she has dark brown eyes. Against my better judgement I want to rush and put my arms around her but I control myself.

"Sorry, we've made you jump," says Dilaver Bey.

"Welcome," I say extending my hand to greet her as if I were the hostess. How silly!

"Thank you for coming to see me," Zeliha Bora says in a slightly hoarse voice as if she might have a cold. Somehow I expected her to have a shrill voice. Now she takes hold of my hand as tightly as I took hers. That's good. I don't like limp hand-shakes at all. We are looking each other over from tip to toe. She looks much calmer than me. Even though I am wearing flat shoes I am unexpectedly a head taller than her.

"I'm glad that you agreed to see me. Thank you so much."

"It's about time I spoke to someone."

She makes a sign for me to sit down as she too takes a seat. We sit opposite each other.

"I'll be around if you need anything," says Dilaver Bey as he leaves the room.

"Thank you."

Zeliha Bora and Nevra Tuna, two women of almost the same age sit looking at each other.

"I enjoy reading your column," she says smiling.

"Thank you."

Zeliha Bora has a slightly Eastern Anatolian accent. The almost negligible twist of her lips gives her a condescending air. We remain silent for a while not knowing what to say next.

"I hope that they're treating you well here," I say more to break the silence than anything else and then I immediately regret saying it. What could I possibly do if she had said no?

"No complaints at all."

"Our meeting wasn't confirmed until yesterday evening. Hasan Bey finally called me last night otherwise I wouldn't have come empty handed... I would have tried to get a few things you might need."

"Thank you. There isn't anything I need. The only thing I want is to be out of here as soon as possible."

"You will, soon. Very, very... soon."

"*Inshallah.*"

"There's a lot of effort being made for you, you know that. Signatures are being gathered, letters written."

"Apparently."

"It's all bound to achieve results."

"*Inshallah.*"

"Zeliha Hanım... We have very little time... You know that a very influential person has arranged this meeting for us... We might not be able to meet again."

"I know."

"Let's get on with it then. First tell me about your childhood, your village, your tribe..."

"If we start that far back we might not have time to get to the reason for me being here."

"We must make room for your life story in the article... It must not be full of political messages."

"But it's my political persuasion that makes me who I am."

"Maybe so, but surely what you went through in your life too must have contributed in forging your political identity."

"In my opinion talking about my childhood will be a waste of our limited time. You must be able to find out all about that from others."

"I still think I should get it from the horse's mouth. For instance I'd like to know how you felt as a child being raised by three mothers. How the tribal customs affected you. Surely only you can explain those feelings."

"You have apparently done your homework well. You seem to know all about my childhood anyway."

"Yes, I know that you come from a large family with many children and that you were brought up by three mothers as an orphan in your tribe."

"So, there you are... we can skip my childhood!"

I realise that I won't be able to overcome her stubbornness. What I really want to hear most are her childhood recollections. Maybe if I leave it for now I might be able to get it out of her later on.

"Fine, let's skip your childhood and go straight on to your youth. Apparently you got married at a very early age. I believe you married someone your family didn't approve of. Then you left your first husband and married someone considerably older than you. Why did you leave your first husband? Did your family push you to it?"

"No, I realised that I had made a mistake and returned home."

"So, the tribe didn't force you?"

"I told you, no one forced me, I returned home of my own free will. We didn't get along."

"Who chose your present husband?"

"My family considered him suitable."

"Wasn't it because they wanted to punish you... I mean... because of your first marriage?"

"Saying that would be an insult to my husband. I've always been very proud to be his wife."

"But isn't there a big age gap?"

"So what! He has treated me very well and has made me happy."

"You didn't marry for love though did you?"

"I was disappointed when I married for love. Arranged marriages work better. Love can develop later some times."

"Zeliha Hanım I am here because I want to write your whole story. In fact I have taken great risks..."

When I see the expression on her face I don't finish my sentence. How can one say 'I have taken great risks for just a few hours interview with you' when that woman has been in prison for years. I clear my throat.

"I want us to talk sincerely without ulterior motives. I want us to analyse the reasons that has put us on opposing sides. Let us first discuss our differences as a Kurd and as a Turk in this country of ours and try to solve them between ourselves. I'd like my article to mirror our conclusions..."

"In other words let's save the world, is that it?"

"Not the entire world... Just our... country... our people."

"You're very optimistic."

"I believe that every problem can be solved by discussing, by understanding each other."

"It would be lovely if it were that easy."

"I may be just an ordinary journalist but I can assure you that there are millions out there who think like me. Many people don't want to quarrel and fight, they don't want to kill and humiliate, they believe that people ought to be free to speak their mother tongue, watch their own TV stations and listen to their own radio programmes. As a journalist I'm simply their voice."

"Where are all these millions of people at election times? How come we always end up with leaders who are backed up by militants and war-mongers then?"

"Zeliha Hanım you had been given a chance to solve the problems in parliament without having to fight and quarrel. Your people made a mistake in not using that opportunity at the time... What I am trying to say is that there are people who make mistakes on both sides."

"So you accept that there are two sides, do you?"

"I believe in one country as a whole. There may be people who speak different languages and have different religions, as in America, but I cannot accept the animosity between them. Especially when resorting to killing and war."

"But both animosity and war are facts of life aren't they? Our homes are raided, villages evacuated and people are humiliated, tortured and killed. There are even those who are burnt in their hotel rooms like kebabs... We have documented every incident."

"Yes Zeliha Hanım you are right. I am personally ashamed for it and have a guilty conscience about all of that but, if you don't mind, I'd like to point out that our villages are being raided too, our men lined up against the wall and shot, houses with elderly people and babies inside raised to the ground. Mines are planted along the roads. Innocent young soldiers in charge of rebuilding roads and buildings are being bombed and teachers are being killed too. Even worse your own people who want no part in these horrible activities are tortured by your warlords, aren't they? All of this is well documented and substantiate with photographs. In a nut-shell, none of us are as pure as driven snow, that's why, with your permission, it would be better not to enter into these accusations. Let's look forward instead. What do you think?"

"Violence and death are natural when fighting for independence."

"By the same token isn't it also natural for a government to defend itself by fighting against such violent actions?"

"It is, but making people eat excrement... That's unacceptable even if your opponent is your fiercest enemy. A community that can accept such a thing has neither honour nor conscience."

"Don't accredit atrocities committed by some perverts to a whole community Zeliha Hanım. Every single person with a sane mind and every institution has vehemently opposed those atrocities. You must not have double standards when talking about community principles. When a policeman is shot right before his child's eyes in the middle of a crowded bazaar and not a single eye-witness comes forward, isn't it fair to say that that community has no conscience either? Do you remember those children who were killed at the foot of Mount Cudi? Unfortunately it was me who had to write the caption for the photograph showing the children's bodies. Do you know how old they were? One of the girls was eight, the other nine and the little boy only three years old. At Bari village, a firing squad lined the men up against the wall of the mosque and shot them all. Are such atrocities part of what you earlier called a war of independence?"

Zeliha Bora's dark eyes flash an expression of animosity.

"Can I ask you something?"

"Feel free."

"On whose behalf are you here?"

"I beg your pardon."

"You came here to see me on behalf of whom? On whose behalf are you going to bark in your column?"

It seems that what I had been afraid of is about to happen. I feel the blood rushing to my head, my ears are burning and my right eye is twitching. I know that right now I will have no control over what comes out of my mouth. That devil inside me has a lot to say and I will eventually find myself scurrying along the corridor towards the exit... and without that all important interview!

"I can assure you that I have not come here on behalf of anybody but myself. I am neither anybody's spokesperson nor anybody's lap dog. I am a journalist and I want to write your life story. I had hoped that as two sensible women speaking face to face we may also have been able to come up with some answers to the existing problems. I'm here of my own choice. I can't even say that my newspaper is behind me. All I will get out of this interview, if it is printed, is my usual fee for my column. I'm not fighting a cause like you. I'm merely a writer, a researcher earning a living. Since you seem determined to turn this dialogue into an 'us and you' issue I want to point out that, for personal reasons, I love you and your people very deeply and furthermore I respect your cause. The difference between us is that I am independent. That's why I can look at this situation in an unbiased way."

A voice inside me tells me, "Don't get on your high horse Nevra, don't make a mess out of this too," but as usual my logic isn't able to make me hold my tongue. I wonder if I will ever listen to reason. Will I ever learn?

"Is it because you respect our cause that you get so irritated and make these accusations?"

I understand that she is becoming as nervous as me from the fact that her Kurdish accent is becoming more pronounced and making her feel uncomfortable. On the other hand it is helping me to relax and calm down.

"What a pity that you can't believe my good intentions! I wonder who has put all this rubbish into your heads, who has fooled you? Why has this issue escalated so badly when it could easily have been solved? How I wish that you could realise that we, as a nation, have no friends except each other. If we can't secure an agreement with each other we only stand to lose."

"Let's not kid ourselves, reporter lady. Are you suggesting that this country is not divided? We both know what we are. We both know what we want. And we both know what we have to do..."

"As I just said, I don't have a mission like you," interrupting her. "You can't easily take the weight off your shoulders. You can't be as independent as I am. You can't really talk about things that are deep in your heart. I forgot that you will surely have to report back every single word that passes between us to your war lord. I'm sorry, I shouldn't have been so insistent after all, you do have to consider your cause."

"Of course I do."

"In that case why don't you talk to me about your mission?"

"The independence... the freedom of my people?"

"Do you think it is right to consider people living in one country as 'us' and 'you'? Doesn't every sensible person want freedom for everyone who lives within our borders?"

"I'm concerned about my people above all else."

"Aren't what you consider your people my people too? Aren't we all sharing the same land?"

"Don't make me laugh!"

"Look, our mother tongues may be different but we've been living on top of one another on the same land Zeliha... Do you mind me calling you by your first name?"

"No, I don't Nevra Hanım... Especially as you like us so much."

I ignore the fact that she is sending me up.

"I'd appreciate it if you'd also drop the Hanım bit, just call me Nevra." She doesn't comment so I continue to speak, "If our people have been able to marry each other, lived peacefully as neighbours and become such good friends..."

"Is that what we've become?" she says sarcastically.

"Well, haven't we?"

"No we haven't!"

"That's not fair. We fought the great war of independence together. Hand in hand, shoulder to shoulder."

"So you acknowledge that do you?"

"Of course, I do. I wholeheartedly believe that with good intentions and with time we can resolve everything. In fact, we are already making headway."

"Oh really!"

"Yes we are."

"Like what for instance?"

"We're about to resolve the language problem."

"Not before time, after all these years of harassment for speaking our mother tongue."

"Only the other week, I was in the Eastern Anatolia and the villages are full of women and children who can't speak Turkish. In fact in some villages there wasn't a single person who spoke Turkish. What language do you think they used?"

"Are you making fun of me Nevra Hanım? I'm sure you understand what I'm saying; I'm sure you realise that I'm talking about our cultural rights. But then, you're all the same. You always manage to come up smelling of roses."

"I know that we've had our faults in the past but now we are trying to repair them."

"You don't even allow us to use the names we choose. For years we couldn't even call our children what we wanted to. Even the name on my birth certificate isn't that chosen by my parents it's the one the registration clerk considered suitable."

I feel a twinge in my heart and have a brief dizzy spell. I suddenly flash back to my childhood but quickly return to the present.

"That was certainly very silly but all these things are in the past."

"Only because of pressure from Europe. If it weren't for this fixation of yours to join the European Community none of the problems would have been solved."

"You've got a point there. Europeans had always some power over us. You rely on them too. Believe in me, these European powers don't help anyone unless there is something in it for them. They may be looking after you now but they are certainly doing it for their own reasons. If they are giving you something today they will definitely want something in return tomorrow. Don't trust them Zeliha Hanım."

"Who should we trust then?"

"Trust your fellow countrymen who are struggling for democracy."

"But they're the ones who shut me up in here."

"Some mistakes will be made along the way but it is important to put them right in the end."

"In other words I am to wait here until someone makes up his mind, is that it?"

"No, certainly not but I think it would be wise for you to wait for the court's decision."

"I thought you said that you hadn't come here in order to fight or threaten me!"

"I didn't threaten you."

"You just did."

"I didn't"

"I have a feeling you're trying to intimidate me. I think you have a hidden agenda which is; 'If you don't do as we say and continue to cause trouble we can bring in restrictions again'."

"Who the hell am I to make such threats? May I ask you what gave you that impression?"

While I am saying this I can't help thinking that obviously no matter what race they are, the people in this land of ours have certainly had more than their fair share of persecution.

"If I knew whose spokesperson you are, I'd be able to tell you."

"Are you all so sceptical?"

"We certainly are, we've suffered a lot."

"Everybody in this country has suffered a lot. We are still suffering. The only thing I want to do is to strengthen friendship amongst our people not animosity."

"Were we ever friends?"

I content myself with a smile.

"You may smile as much as you like. You can even laugh. I wish I could after all I'm the victim, the prisoner here. As for you you're unjust, powerful and free."

I am hurt when I realise she has misinterpreted my smile. In fact I'm angry.

"Your considering yourself the victim doesn't mean that you are 100% right you know, Zeliha Hanım."

We have both raised our voices; we stand up hands planted firmly on the table and lean our heads toward each other like two roosters preparing for a fight. We look at each other with daggers in our eyes. Neither of us understands what the other is saying because we are both shouting at the same time.

"Get out of here; I don't have to explain anything to you!"

"I haven't asked for explanations. I came here for an interview."

"Well you won't get one that's for sure! Get out!"

"You're sending me away, but don't forget that we have never sent you Kurds away, we have only wanted to live alongside the lot of you. We have elected members of parliament, ministers and prime ministers from amongst you. We have even had you as commanders in the army. There have been professors, pop-singers, folk singers, writers and intellectuals. There have been very rich people amongst you even mafia godfathers. We have never even considered you different from 'us'. Why then when you were in a position to achieve everything did you try to separate yourselves from us? Tell me why Zeliha?"

"You'd better get this into your heads. This land is not only yours; it's ours as well and please don't tell me that you wouldn't like to get rid of us. Firstly, I'm sure you realise you couldn't have sent us away from our own land and secondly, we never wanted to be 'us' or 'you'; we have always wanted to be our own selves, speak and write our own language."

"You could have earned that right without resorting to terrorism. You could have earned that right in the Assembly which you have exploited since the day you entered it."

"Nevra Hanım it's very clear to me that we will never be able to get along. Let's end this interview here and now!"

"We can get along. We are obliged to. Especially, you and me. We are two people who love each other. As friends, we must be able to at least discuss these issues."

"Excuse me, did you say 'two people who love each other'? Where did that come from?"

Zeliha Bora pushes her chair back and stands up. I get up quickly and rush to the door in order to stop her leaving. I lean against the door and stretch my arms out across the doorway.

"Will you get out of my way? This interview is over Nevra Hanım."

"Zeliha..."

For an instant, her hand freezes on the doorknob.

"Don't leave Zelo, please don't!"

Her face blanches as if she has seen a ghost. She leans against the wall to steady herself.

"Doesn't my name ring a bell? Don't you remember we were once the best of friends?"

She pulls herself together and is looking at me angrily.

"We have never been friends and we will never be either! Get out of my way before I call someone."

I still have my arms stretched across the doorway and I don't budge an inch.

"Zeliha, look at me carefully. Look into my eyes. My hair wasn't this colour when I was younger; it was light brown. I had it tied in two plaits; my mother used to tie the ends with red-spotted ribbons. I had given them to you before we left Sarıcadam."

The anger in her face turns to confusion. She looks straight into my eyes briefly.

"I had even left my bunny-rabbit with you so that you wouldn't forget me."

"Nevo?!"

"Of course, Nevo. Nevra Leventoğlu; I was the district officer's daughter."

All of a sudden, we are in each other's arms. We are standing in front of the door hugging each other tightly and swaying from side to side as if we are one. The tears running from my eyes drop on to her shoulder. I can't see her face but I can tell that she's crying too from the way her body is shaking.

I'm stroking her hair. She pushes me away gently and looks at me through tearful eyes. Then, we start to laugh. We are standing hugging each other the tears streaming down our cheeks and laughing and crying at the same time.

NEVO & ZELO

We're in each other's arms. We're standing by the van hugging each other tightly and swaying from side to side as if we are one. The tears running from my eyes drop on to my friend's shoulder. I can't see her face but I can tell she is crying too from the way her body is shaking.

"Come on children, that's enough, we've got to catch the train," says my father.

"Please father, can't Zelha come with us?"

"You know very well that's not possible."

"Why not?"

"Zelha's mother wouldn't let her go just as I wouldn't let you go," says my mother.

"But she doesn't have just one mother, she has lots of them."

"Even more reason... If one doesn't let her go the others won't either. Come on now, time to go or we'll miss our train."

When I can't get my own way with my mother I turn again to my father.

"If she stays in her village she won't be able to go to school and they'll marry her off."

"Don't be silly my pet. She's only a child."

"But, don't you know dad, the girls in Zelha's farm are always made to marry while they are still very young?"

My father affectionately tries to separate us and strokes Zelha's hair.

"She won't be getting married for a long time yet," he says, "and you'll be writing to each other very often. Let us know if you should have any problems my dear, won't you? Don't forget you're part of our family; you're our little girl too. We'll never forget you."

Our suitcases and parcels are loaded in to the back of the van. A lump sticks in my throat as the inevitable moment approaches in spite of my attempts to prolong our goodbyes. Three times I pretended that I needed to go to the lavatory, each time Zelha came running indoors with me. We hugged each other over and over again promising all sorts of things. Eventually, I ran out of excuses. My mother has been given the paper bags filled with wild thyme by Zelha's mothers. The fine lace embroidered and knitted slippers they meticulously made have been handed over as parting gifts and loaded on the back of the van too. One of her mothers, the one we all call Kader Ana, insists on giving my father some freshly baked bread for the journey despite his protests. At the last minute, we share out the photographs taken by the sergeant the summer before. It's then that I notice that Zelha's plaits are tied with the red-dotted ribbon I had given her the previous evening and she is wearing the patent leather shoes my father had given to her for the last bayram. We finally hug each other one last time.

"I'll never forget you," I say. "You're my most beloved friend. My blood-sister."

"You're all these things to me too," says Zelha. "Don't forget you promised to write often."

"Promise."

"Come on you two," says my father trying to pull me away by the arm. "Get into the van."

We're finally separated. I climb up into the van snivelling and sit next to my mother. Abbas Efendi places the rabbit cage between my feet. Just as he is about to close the door I shout, "Stop! Stop!"

"What now?" asks the driver.

I step down and pick up the rabbit's cage.

"Here you are Zelo. I want to leave Çin-Çin with you."

"What an excellent idea," says my mother. "Why on earth didn't we think of that before?" She seems to be delighted to get rid of the rabbit.

"Please let me know how he's getting on when you write."

"But my writing is not as pretty as yours."

"Doesn't matter, just keep writing."

"I will Nevo, I will."

God only knows how many times we repeated ourselves making the same promises over and over again. We're now hugging each other one more time.

Finally, we set off on our way as the assembled crowd applauded and waved. Some of them pour buckets of water after us, a tradition to ensure a safe journey. I lean out of the van's side window to wave goodbye and scream at the top of my voice, "Eze te tu jar ji bir nekim, Zelo!" "I'll never forget you Zelo!"

Zelha, crying with a runny nose, is standing holding the rabbit's cage in her patent leather shoes, her flannelette trousers and her green and orange striped sweater. I know that her soul is still with us although her silhouette is getting smaller and smaller as it recedes into the distance. She is not yet aware of the seeds of change that have been planted in her as a result of having lived as a member of the district officer's family and attending school. Wanting to marry someone she will love instead of becoming a wife in a polygamous household is just one example. As for me, I feel deeply with the innocence of a child that a part of me snapped off and remained in Saricadam. I know through some strange premonition that I will never again find a place where humans and animals live in such harmony with nature, a place where the people are so pure and innocent. That's why I feel a pain in my heart.

"Enough is enough young lady, sit down and close the window," says my father. "I can assure you that you will make lots of friends wherever you go. If you behave like this every time, you are parted from one of them we are really in for trouble!"

I leave my heart behind in Sarıcadam as we drive away and cry all the way to the station. I was to learn later that Zelha, who had desperately tried to control herself in front of us, finally broke down crying and screaming until her voice became hoarse.

We sit together holding hands for a long time. We must both be thinking of the days when, according to the season, we were either covered in mud or chasing goats, sheep, squirrels and butterflies. The days when we almost disappeared amongst the reeds by the stream and blended with nature as if we had become wild grass ourselves. I'm the first one to break the silence.

"Do you know Zelha, whenever I am bored or distressed my mind flashes back to Sarıcadam like a shooting star? When I think of those days, I feel better. In my dreams I often see us running along the stream. That helps me to sleep more peacefully. I'm so happy that his superiors appear to have forgotten my father out there at the beginning of his career."

"When someone is posted to such a remote location, they are often forgotten."

I find myself searching for Zelha's hands roughened while climbing trees and collecting pine-cones. Instead, I find that the hand I am holding in mine is really soft. I turn her hand over and look at her index finger.

"You won't find the scar," she says, "It disappeared a few months after you left."

"Do you remember how my mother got into a flap worrying that we might get infected?"

"And she worried in vain because nothing happened."

"One of your mothers had an alternative cure if you remember. She spread some honey on our fingers."

"Yes it was Cevahir Ana who knew all about that sort of thing."

"Can you imagine how stupid we were to try to become blood-sisters using a nail instead of a needle to pierce our skin?"

"But we chose the nail deliberately so that our sisterhood would be sealed more strongly. So that we would never part."

"And didn't it work Zelo? Look, here we are together again after all these years."

I can't help stroking my childhood friend's hair.

"Did you know it was me when you came here?" asks Zelha.

"It would be a lie if I said I didn't. I must admit that I had suspicion television coverage and press photographs can be misleading. Your surname and tribe are different now so I couldn't really be sure. Time and time again I tried to imagine how you might appear now by looking at our childhood photos. You always had a big smile on your face in all of the pictures we had taken together, so your eyes looked like slits. As if that wasn't enough in most of them your front teeth were missing. I still couldn't be sure when I compared our photos with those in the papers. How did I expect to, a whole lifetime had passed by? You have changed quite a bit Zelha. Your hair is lighter, it's almost auburn now, and I remember it as jet-black. Oh, how I envied the shine on your hair. Your surname has changed as has your accent and of course you have grown but your eyes... your eyes are just the same. I recognised you the moment you walked in."

"Why didn't you tell me at once?"

"I was dumbstruck. I was going to tell you eventually... Anyway what about you? You didn't recognise me at all did you?"

"No, not at all. I can't believe I didn't, shame on me!"

"Have I changed so much more than you over the years?"

"You were quite plump then and now you're so slim."

"It was you who were slim then and considerably taller than me."

"But look at you now Nevo, you're much taller than me. Your father must have watered you well. Speaking of which, how are your parents? Both well, I hope."

"My father retired a long time ago. He's living in Urla now. I lost my mother last year."

"Oh no! I'm so sorry. What happened?" Zelha has tears in her eyes.

"Cancer."

"What a beautiful young woman your mother was. In spite of all the years that have passed I can still remember my very first sight of her. Mother and I were sent to your house and it was your mother who opened the door to us when we got there. She was wearing a pink dressing gown, her long hair rested on her shoulders. Her eyes were emerald green. Up to that day I had only seen dark skinned people with brown eyes in the village. So bewildered I was that I wanted to touch her peachy skin."

I couldn't believe my eyes either when I first saw Zelha arrive with her mother Kader. Even now I still remember how startled I was, in spite of my young age, when I first saw her jet black hair and eyes. She was wearing a long red dress made of shiny velvet, black stockings and dark grey galoshes. It was obvious that she had chosen to wear her best dress for the visit. She had taken off the galoshes outside the door and then her shoes in the hall. Kader Ana gave her daughter a pair of hand-knitted slippers to wear and gave me a pair as well. When they caught me looking at Zelha's slippers out of the corner of my eye, Zelha had said something to her mother in a language I didn't understand. Kader Ana then asked me if I wanted the pair Zelha was wearing. I shook my head to show that I didn't because the slippers she had given me were knitted in shades of my favourite colour, blue.

"Look Nevra," my mother had said to me, "This little girl's name is Zelha. She came to play with you so that you won't get bored when you are on your own. Why don't you hold her hand and take her to your room to see your toys?" I had stood still trying to hide myself in the folds of my mother's dressing gown. The girl standing in front of me didn't look anything like any of my previous friends.

Her mother had tried to encourage her to step forward when she saw that I wasn't moving. The little girl had approached me taking hold of my hand slowly.

"Nave min Zelha," she said in that strange language.

"What did she say?" I asked my mother.

"She told you her name, why don't you tell her yours?"

"Nevra."

She had given me a wide smile exposing her brilliant white teeth then she spoke to me again.

"What did she say this time?"

"She is asking you to take her to your room," Kader Ana had translated.

"What language is that?"

"She is speaking her own language. I'm sure you'll learn each other's languages while you play together," my mother had replied.

"That's right," Kader Ana had added.

I had taken her to my room as if I were in a trance and laid out all of my toys in front of her. There were several dolls in multi-coloured dresses. There was a cradle, a pram, a little oven, some kitchen utensils, even a miniature iron and ironing board. Zelha scrutinised everything muttering in her own language as she did so. What she had appeared to be most interested in were the modern clothes the dolls were wearing which were so different from her own. Then she had started to play with the dolls miming to me that we were to be mothers with their babies. We had had a short argument over the doll's names because she didn't like the names I had given them. We finally agreed about the names but she was certainly in charge. For instance she was setting out the china on a cloth she had laid on the floor not on the table as I did. Several times she threw the twigs and leaves I pretended were food on to the floor saying, "Na, na." When we couldn't communicate with sign language we rushed off to Kader Ana who told her in Kurdish that the food was to be eaten at the table. She then translated Zelha's response which was that, "Food is to be eaten on the cloth on the floor." I insisted for God knows how long but she argued vehemently in both Kurdish and Turkish and eventually I gave up and transferred what was on the table to the floor. She was much quicker than me at picking up another language. As for me, it seemed that I was bewitched by those black magnetic eyes of hers. She was so very different from me. I was totally willing to enter into her world which was both foreign and interesting to me. I was immediately prepared to do whatever she asked me to do. I pretended to be breast-feeding the dolls by pressing them to my chest or feeding them with a spoon. Rocking them to sleep in my lap and then laying them side by side on the floor and covering them up. While I was carrying out her instructions she sat on my bed watching and directing me in her own language.

By the end of the day, my mother too had submitted totally to Kader Ana's wishes and managing abilities. She had stayed in bed all day and eaten whatever Kader Ana had placed in front of her. It was as though this mother and daughter possessed some powers that made others give in to them. When my father had come home in the evening I enthusiastically reported every detail to him. "The daughter of the maid who came to us today doesn't speak Turkish, Dad, but we had so much fun," I had said.

"Kader Hanım isn't a maid," he had protested. "She is only coming to help your mother who is unwell."

"Is Mum ill Dad?"

"No she isn't but she mustn't tire herself. Kader Hanım will be taking care of the housework for some time." Then turning to my mother, "For goodness sake, Nermin please make sure that our neighbours realise that Kader Hanım isn't a maid. It would be awful if she got the wrong impression," he had said.

My mother had been surprised. "But aren't we going to pay her anything?" she had asked.

"I did insist but Sadık Ağa adamantly refused my offer. The only way to handle this situation is to buy the child some clothes and give the mother an appropriate present," my father had replied.

I wasn't old enough at the time to differentiate between paid, and unpaid help. I had found out later that my mother had suffered several haemorrhages when she had a miscarriage at the end of an eight-month pregnancy and lost the baby. The doctors had recommended that she should rest and my father had asked Sadık Ağa if he knew of a suitable person who could help with the housework. He had responded by suggesting that one of the women from his own household could help the officer's wife. Of course, my father hadn't accepted but the Ağa did insist. His farm was full of women who had nothing else to do but to look after the children and gossip all day long. He had assured my father that one of them would be more useful to him than sitting in the barn and bickering with the others all day long. Kader Ana spoke some Turkish and she had some experience in midwifery. As for Zelha she was the bonus that came with the package for me. This tribeswoman and her daughter brought colour and joy to our calm peaceful household.

In the autumn of that year Zelha had managed to learn Turkish, and we started to go to school together. Zelha would spend the week with us sharing my bedroom and then go with her mother to their village at weekends. When the weather started getting warmer they invited me to their farm. At first I would just go for the day but in time I started spending the night with them as well. I was so happy and had so much fun at the village that my parents couldn't object to my staying there over the weekends.

Kader Ana, Zelha and I would leave school and go to the village on Fridays just like boarding school students, and return home on Sunday evenings. My relationship with Zelha developed into a very special friendship as she described every minute detail of life in her village. She showed me every hill, valley and stream. She taught me to love the trees and nature to such an extent that I felt part of it. She taught me how to lay tables and beds on the floor. She told me about the extra wives called "*kuma*" in polygamous households. She made me understand how it was possible for fathers to have several wives and for children to have several mothers. She also taught me that it was possible for parents to love their own children and their step-children in many different ways just as it was possible for children to love their various parents differently. Most importantly Zelha was my very special friend who helped me to experience limitless happiness as well as the unbearable pain of separation. In short she taught me to appreciate love, life and nature.

We hug each other yet again.

"You eventually had a little brother..."

"That's right, Orhan. I had written to you about that."

"Where's he now?"

"He lives in America. If you had answered my letters we would have known what was going on in each other's lives. Why didn't you answer my letters Zelha?"

"How can you say that? I always replied by return of post."

"Liar!"

"It was only when your rabbit died that it took me ages to pluck up the courage to write, but eventually I did while crying my eyes out."

"I cried a lot, too, when I received that letter. Didn't the poor rabbit fall off the roof?"

"Yes. You must remember Sülü who was a bit half-witted. One day he decided to take the rabbit up on the roof. He opened the cage and the poor thing fell off the edge." Zelha can't help laughing when she remembers, "I gave that idiot such a beating because he wasn't even able to look after a rabbit properly."

"Wasn't it strange how that rabbit became like our mutual child who bonded us together. When it died our communications stopped."

"Not at all. We continued writing to each other after that, too."

"I remember that I didn't get any letters from you after my father was posted to the West. I wrote so many times asking you to come to Urla for your summer holidays."

"I never got those letters. Obviously mother hid them from me."

"Really! Why?"

"Well, I desperately wanted to finish primary school but, as you know, there wasn't a fourth form in our village school. I presume my mothers felt that you might persuade me to come and stay with you so they hid your letters from me."

"But your uncle had promised my father that he would educate you..."

"Don't believe everything you hear. Who keeps those sorts of promises in a village like ours? What's even worse is that I was the only girl in the whole village who wanted to continue her education, so unfortunately I stayed at home and worked in the fields and vineyards with my mothers."

"Do you mean to say that you didn't go to school after the third year?"

"Well I did study at home and eventually took the exam to finish primary school. I have the diploma to prove it so don't you dare look down on me."

"Look down on you? I can assure you that I have always been in awe of you ever since we first met Zelo."

"Don't exaggerate. Why should you be in awe of me?"

"You were always extremely clever, that's why. I had realised that you had special talents even at that early age."

"If you could see that back then you must have special talents, too. Dearest Nevo, I strongly believe that neither brains nor beauty count in this world, what really matters is luck. It seems that mine has run out."

"I can assure you my dear that I don't have much luck either."

"And yet you are so beautiful. No wonder my grandmother always said, 'May God give you the luck bestowed on the ugly ones'. I wonder if we were born ugly we would have been luckier."

"Maybe if we were ugly we might have tried harder to improve ourselves and that might have paved the way to success."

"I certainly tried very hard and look where that got me?"

"Tried? When?"

"When I moved to Ankara with my husband Şiyar, I decided to try to get a secondary school diploma there. You should have seen me then Nevo! I tried so hard even though I was a grown up woman by then. When our children came home from school I sat down to study with them. They'd study for their exams and I'd sit up all night with my history and geography books. I wasn't very good at maths so Şiyar got me a private tutor. I was really determined to succeed. It became an obsession and ultimately I got the diploma I wanted."

"Don't tell me you went on to university too."

"No, for God's sake not that far."

"But with your tenacity it wouldn't have surprised me, Zelo."

"I don't have time for such things any more. I've got other things to accomplish now."

"Really! So tell me how you spend your time nowadays."

"For a start, there's all my correspondence. I read every letter that is sent to me and reply to most of them. There are loads of books that I've got to read, I devote at least two hours each day to reading. Unfortunately, I also have other things on my plate, so I can't always read as much as I'd like to."

"What other things?"

"Things concerning the organisation..."

"Don't try to tell me that all your struggles were for nothing."

"No but all that effort to get diplomas hasn't really affected my life."

"How could it not?"

"For instance, I've always wanted to be a teacher."

"I do remember. You always wanted me to be the student and you the teacher when we played school together."

"Do you know why that was?"

"Why?"

"Because I was taller than you and teachers should be taller than their students."

"But not at universities."

"For goodness sake woman how was I supposed to know about universities at that age?"

"I think you still can become a teacher, Zelo."

"No I don't want that any more, I have other fish to fry these days."

"Shall I tell you something? I believe that not only could you become a teacher but you could be anything else that you set your mind to because you're both clever and patient."

"Thank you."

"It wasn't meant as a compliment."

"I know that."

"Since you have time to read while you are in here why don't you apply for an Open University course to study a subject of your own choice?"

"Don't be ridiculous, Nevo."

"Why do you say that? In my opinion, it must have been more difficult to take the primary and secondary school exams without having attended classes. You managed that so you could easily graduate from university. Honestly, Zelo, I would if I were in your shoes. In any case weren't you saying that you were reading a lot."

"People like me who have been accused of being separatists can't work as civil servants. You should know that. What's more, I have graduated from the university of life, Nevo. In my opinion, that's the best university. I started there when I was fifteen and I'm still learning. I'll become a professor soon."

When I realised that there was nothing more to say on the matter I got up and picked up my bag from where I had left it. I took out my cigarette lighter, lit two cigarettes and offered her one. She took it without hesitation. I sat down opposite her again. She took hold of the lighter and was scrutinizing it.

"They must have thought that this was your lipstick otherwise they would have confiscated it."

"If you like it you can have it."

"No, no I couldn't."

"Why not? Keep it as a momento from me," I said pushing the lighter towards her. She didn't argue. She took it and put it in her pocket.

"Where are we to put the ash?" she asked, looking around for an ashtray.

She was rather tidy like this as a child, too. She used to get down on her hands and knees to pick up bread and biscuit crumbs that I had carelessly dropped on the floor.

"Why don't you just drop the ash on the stone floor Zelha, it won't do it any harm."

We took several puffs without speaking then, "Did they make you get married very early?" I asked.

"They didn't make me marry anyone Nevo, I ran away."

"What? I can't believe this! You ran away, with whom?"

"Alişan, do you remember Alişan?"

"Wasn't he one of the boys we used to play with down by the stream?"

"Wasn't he just! Do you remember the day I fell into the stream?"

"How can I forget it?"

"Well, he was the one who jumped into the water to rescue me."

"Oh yes, of course. Tallish with bright blue eyes."

"That's him alright. He became very handsome as he grew up. You should have seen him."

"They used to live in the thatched cottage behind your farm didn't they?"

"That's right, his father used to guard our fields. Well that's who I ran away with."

"I can't believe your courage. They could have shot you for that. How the hell did you get away with it?"

"They say love is blind, Nevo. I was only fifteen, I was in love. I begged my uncle to let me marry Alişan but, he wouldn't hear of it."

"Why?"

"He claimed that Alişan was after my money, as if I had any. How could a girl without a father have money, I ask you? Anyway, he didn't give in. Money or no money, I was a girl of the tribe and I should marry someone of his choosing."

"What about your mothers, didn't they back you up?"

"Do you think that the women there had a say in such matters? Especially those without a husband. My mother begged my uncle, but he insisted that he would find the right man for me. In my opinion, he was more interested in the dowry he could get out of me."

"As if he needed it, so how did you get away?"

"Don't ask. It wasn't easy at all. It was I who pleaded with Alişan to elope after I had seen the man my uncle had chosen for me. He was much older than me with a huge nose. He was balding and what hair he had on the sides of his head was grey. He visited us at the farm loaded with presents in the summer of my fifteenth birthday. He brought fine materials and slippers for my mothers and bracelets for me. I was made to serve him coffee. As I bent forward to serve him I staggered back from the stench of cigarettes that emanated from him. He smelled like an ashtray. When I spoke to my mother about it all she said was, 'All men smell like ashtrays.' 'My grandfather and uncles don't stink like that,' I said kicking and stamping. 'You're used to their smell and you'll get used to his smell too,' she said. When I couldn't get anywhere with my mother I went to Cevahir Ana and then to aunt Satı. All three must have been so pleased with their presents that they didn't want to know about my protests. I quickly realised that none of them would back me up. Maybe Makbule Ana would back me up because, she was still very young herself but she was no longer living at the farm with us. I had no other choice than to run away. Alişan had received his call up papers and was to report for his military service by the end of the month. We came to the conclusion that if we were to elope while he was in the army, they wouldn't put the blame on him. They wouldn't shoot him because they would think that I had run away with somebody else."

"Why should they think that?"

"Well, you don't suppose Alişan would have been able to hide me under his bunk while he was in the army do you?"

"You're probably right."

"I also threatened my mother by saying, 'If you force me to get married I'll run away to a big city and find work. You'll never find me then.' 'Who do you think you are,' she said. 'Just because you learned to read and write don't think you know it all. Are you going to become a prostitute?' 'I can become a cleaner or look after children,' I replied hoping to change the subject. But she came back at me with, 'Wouldn't it be better if you stayed at home like a good woman and looked after your husband rather than strangers?' Then, she went on and on telling me how lucky I was that such a wealthy man wanted me and how much the dowry he was offering amount to. 'Don't sacrifice me mother for the sake of a few sheep,' I pleaded. 'What are you talking about? A few sheep, a few sheep! I wouldn't even give our guard-dog for that,' she snapped. 'Listen to me my girl. I beg you not to be so foolish. This man will give us land and gold which will save us both from being totally dependent on your uncles. We wouldn't need them anymore,' she pleaded again. 'We could both leave and enjoy the comforts of our new home.' I hadn't realised until then that she was thinking of moving out with me to save herself from the constant bickering and the clutches of my grandmother, poor thing. 'We will at least have a man to take care of us.' 'I'll work and look after you Mum,' I said to her. 'But isn't it so much better to be the lady of your own house?' she said. 'Why are you so against my working? Didn't you yourself have to work for the district officer, once?' I asked. 'That wasn't the same,' she replied indignantly. 'Why not?' I asked, 'a servant is a servant.' That was when she slapped me across my face as if with a sledge-hammer. She had never hit me since I was twelve, I can't tell you how hurt I was. I ran to my room crying and didn't eat with the family for days. I only ate what Hediye brought me secretly. I also sent word to Alişan that I would commit suicide if he didn't find a way out. I had no such intentions but I just wanted him to get a move on. I wasn't sure that I could cope with the pressure that my mothers and uncles would put on me while he was in the army. I simply wanted to hasten our elopement."

"I can't believe your guts."

"The impetuosity of youth I suppose."

"So what did you do while he was in the army then? Did you really look after kids or what?"

"No, of course not. One of Alişan's uncles had settled in Mersin so we first went there when we eloped. We stayed in his uncle's house for three nights. We were so scared that we couldn't even look out of the window. Then he went to report for duty and I stayed on with the uncle and waited for Alişan's return."

"How was the uncle?.. I mean, did he treat you well?

"He had three daughters around my age. Two of them were going to school and the third stayed at home. I helped her with the housework. They were very kind to me. God bless them."

"So exactly how did you get away from your village? All your men always carry guns."

"Things worked out well for us... It was the beginning of summer... I'm sure you remember the Sürmeli family; their daughter was getting married so they had organised the henna night to take place at their house in the vineyard. Everybody was invited. The day before the party, I pretended that I had diarrhoea and yet was very eager to go. My poor mother felt so sorry for me. That morning she cooked rice soup to stop my runny stomach and she kept on giving me strong tea, too... 'You come along but don't stuff yourself like a goose,' she advised. In the afternoon, my mothers and I, the aunts, girls and children, we all crammed on to the back of a lorry and went to the henna ceremony. What a rigmarole that was; you should have seen it. While food was served on one side, drums and horns were played on the other, all the girls were dancing. The bride's trousseau was displayed on a table and the women gathered around to inspect and comment on it. In other words everyone was so involved in their own thing that they were not aware of what was going on elsewhere. I kept on running to the loo pretending to still be ill. I'd stay away for a while and then return to my mother's side.

In the meantime, you won't believe me if I tell you that I really started to have pains in my stomach. Just about then they began to play the music signalling the start of the wedding. The female relatives holding candles in their hands escorted the bride. Everybody ran towards them. Alişan was to send his nephew riding a motorcycle to the gate at the end of the back garden. I took advantage of the commotion to make my escape. 'Where are you going?' my mother shouted after me. 'To the loo,' I replied. 'For goodness sake, can't you hold on to it for a minute?' she asked. 'Can't you wait at least until they have burnt the henna? Is it that urgent?' 'OK,' I said reluctantly. Well, the henna was burnt and the ritual painting of the girls' hands done. I started to feel on edge. I wanted this ceremony to end but the singing went on and on. Eventually I also had to have my hands hennaed. And do you know what Nevo? While they were applying the burnt henna to my hands, a sad thought crossed my mind. 'That's it,' I thought, I won't ever be able go through this ceremony. I won't be all dressed up on the back of a horse riding to my husband's house accompanied by drums and horns and a cheering crowd. That traditional gold coin necklace won't be placed around my neck. Nobody will give me their blessing... But, on the other hand if I wanted these things so badly I would have to sacrifice waking up in the morning by the side of the man I loved and marry an old man who smelt like an ashtray. When I thought of Zülfükar, the man who wanted to marry me, his face and smell, I rushed to the loo. I went in and out like a shot and started to run towards the back garden. I jumped over the lowest part of the wall and there was Binali waiting for me with his motorcycle hidden behind a tree. As I ran towards him, I could see that is face was ashen with anxiety.

'There you are,' he said, 'I was beginning to think you won't be able to make it. What took you so long?'

'My mother was watching me like a hawk, Binali,' I said. 'I was waiting for the right time.'

'I swear Alişan would have killed me if I had returned without you.'

'Well, I'm here now.'

'You're sure, aren't you?' he asked, 'no going back?'

'No.'

'Fine, but if you change your mind or get caught you've never seen me, OK? You just ran away on your own, is that clear?'

'Perfectly.'

'Promise?'

'Promise.'

'I want you to swear to it.' Obviously, he was as scared as me of our tribe but I suppose that his pride would not allow him to let Alişan down.

'I swear to God, *Vallahi Billahi*, I shall tell them that I jumped over the wall and ran all the way to where the buses are,' I reassured him.

'Hop up behind me and put your arms around my waist,' he said hurriedly.

I got on the back seat of the motorbike and off we went. I had neither a bundle nor a bag with me. I didn't even have a spare set of underwear. That's how I ran away to Alişan. My hands were dyed with henna alright but I had nothing else. The only thing I had taken with me from the house was my birth certificate and that was only because Alişan had insisted that I should. 'If you take your birth certificate with you they will think that you have run away to get married and, since I'm with the army, they'll think you ran away with somebody else and will leave me alone,' he had warned."

"Thank God, you took your birth certificate with you."

"Yes, but even that wasn't easy to get. I can't tell you what I had to go through to get it from my uncle. He used to keep all his documents like deeds and birth certificates in the office room which was on the north side of the farmhouse. You know that room don't you?"

"I remember it well."

"One night when everybody was asleep I took a torch and went to that room. My heart was beating like a drum. I knew that the key was hidden in a lidded bowl so I took the key immediately and opened the cupboard and rummaged through the drawers. Everything else was there, deeds, tax receipts, letters written in the old Ottoman script but damn it, there were no birth certificates! I slumped to the floor and rested against the table leg holding my tears back and thinking, 'There's nothing else I can do, I'll have to leave without it.' I collected all the papers that had fallen on the floor one by one checking again. Not there! Not there! I put everything back in the drawer, closed the cupboard door and locked it. Just as I was about to put the key back in the bowl I heard footsteps outside. I switched off the torch, knelt down on the floor and waited. 'My God,' I whispered to myself, 'What can I say if I am found here with a torch in my hand?' I rolled the torch away on the kilim and held my breath and stayed like that without a sound. And just then, what do you think happens? I want to sneeze don't I? I covered my mouth with my scarf until I was nearly choking. If you asked me Nevo, I couldn't tell you how long I stayed like that. I might say a lifetime and I wouldn't even argue with you if you said a thousand years. Then, just as the footsteps came they went away. I sighed with relief as I tried to stretch my legs. I'm all stiff, I can't straighten my back and I'm covered in sweat."

"The suspense is killing me. Go on, get to the point. Did you manage to get out of there without getting caught?"

"Not getting caught is one thing, not finding my birth certificate another..."

"For God's sake, get on with it. What happened next?"

"I decided to leave without the certificate. Just as I was walking to the door, I remembered the small drawer in the table that was never locked, so I decided to go back and check it."

"Don't tell me it was there all the time?"

"Yes, it was there alright, Nevo."

"Unbelievable!"

"I was flabbergasted. I had opened the drawer to find an old newspaper my grandfather must have left there for some reason. I fumbled around under the paper and there they were, all of our birth certificates. I turned on the torch and found my own, I pressed it to my heart, closed the drawer and switched off the torch. But I couldn't just walk out and leave. Do you know what I felt at that moment with my birth certificate pressed against my chest? I felt that for the first time ever I had taken my life into my own hands and I could command my own destiny. My knees were knocking and tears of joy were streaming down my cheeks. The certificate that I thought was locked away was right there in my hand. That was all long before my eighteenth birthday. Of course, I learnt with time that my life and particularly my future would never be in the palms of my hands. Simply holding on to a birth certificate is not really enough to make you feel free and in control of your life."

"I've got a certificate, too, now," Zelha had said.

We were sitting on the floor with the groundsheet we used as a table cloth pulled on to our laps and eating the pancakes that Kader Ana was serving straight from the stove.

"What do you mean a certificate?"

She had run to the next room and returned with her certificate.

"Oh, I see, you mean your birth certificate."

"Yes, that's right," she said proudly.

"Didn't you have one before?"

"May God bless your father. It's thanks to him that I have got it at all. Apparently, he persuaded my grandpa that since I am going to school now and will soon be getting my primary school diploma I would need it. Not only that but maybe later on when I would marry I would also need it. Grandpa told my uncles and here it is."

I remember taking my friend's birth certificate in my hands and examining it closely.

"But, Zelo, they appear to have mis-spelt your name. Look!"

"What's wrong with it?"

"Your name isn't Zeliha is it?"

"No, it's Zelha."

"Look at this, they've written Zeliha here."

She grabbed it from me and read it carefully.

"You're right! Oh dear, Mum come and have a look at this they've got my name wrong," she called out to her mother.

Her mother had checked the birth certificate once again.

"What's wrong with it darlin'?" she had said pretending to be able to read it. "They've written Zeliha instead of Zelha."

"So what? Zelha, Zeliha what's the difference? It's all the same to me."

"No it isn't auntie Kader, they've inserted an 'i' in her name, that's what's wrong," I said cockily.

"Stop carping on you two after all, I'm your mother and that's the name I chose for you. In our accent it's Zelha, in Turkish its Zeliha, so what?"

"But Mum wasn't my great-grandmother called Zelha?"

"If I had known what an obstinate cow she'd turn out to be I'd never have called you that," said Kader Ana. "Anyway they wrote it right darlin', thank God."

"So, am I to call her Zeliha from now on then?" I asked.

"Call her what you like as long as you don't call her late for her dinner. Don't make things worse than they already are you little madam!"

"My name is Zelha," Zelha had insisted.

"OK, have it your own way, that's what they call you anyway darlin'." Kader Ana had responded as she picked up our plates and dashed off to the kitchen.

When I had returned home I had asked my father about this business of the missing "i".

"Don't stir things up Nevra," my father had replied. "In Turkish the name is spelt with an 'i'. Is that understood my dear!"

When he saw me scowling at him he continued, "It's spelt as Zeliha but pronounced Zelha. It's the same as her calling you Nevro or whatever it is that she calls you…"

"She calls me Nevo."

"There you are then, every region has its own pronunciation, and names can be pronounced differently by different people."

"But Dad…"

"Full stop! End of argument!" My father had replied angrily. "I've got work to do so that's enough."

ZELHA

"Is your name still spelt incorrectly on your birth certificate?"

"Yes," she replied, "but I'm used to it by now. I can't be bothered to make a fuss about it any more. I'm called Zeliha in the city and Zelha in the village. I feel as if I have a split personality. Who knows, maybe I do, Nevo. The real Zelha is somewhere inside me at the moment. The one here talking to you in prison is Zeliha. When the lights are switched off at night and I am alone I ask myself, 'What am I doing here?' Then a voice from deep inside me tells me that it is Zeliha not Zelha lying here. Those responsible for adding the 'i' to my name are the ones who have put me here. When I think like that I can relax a bit. I know that the day will come when I will be Zelha again. I'll return home to my village. I'll take off these town clothes, wear my floral print dress, cover my head with a scarf and sit cross-legged on my divan. Only then will I be able to take on the mantle of being

Zelha again. Don't think for a moment that the only person who affected my life is the clerk who mis-spelt my name. I believe that I was born at the wrong time and in the wrong place. I seem to have come into this world to be at the beck and call of others. It's as though there is no me, there's only someone trying always to do what others want her to do..."

"Dearest Zelo," I interjected sincerely. "I wonder if by changing that single letter in your name we have triggered off the change in you."

"No, my fate was written across my forehead long before that, Nevo. Being born into a tribe in Saricadam, my father dying while I was still very young, meeting you and your family, eloping with Alişan, returning back to my tribe and then marrying my present husband, all of this was pre-ordained."

"I don't think that meeting us was important enough to have been written on your forehead."

"How can you say that, Nevo? Would I have become the same person if I hadn't met you and your family? If I hadn't stayed in your home and not gone to the town school with you. Oh no, Nevo. I would have been married off by the time I was thirteen, before I even had time to learn to read and write properly. Would I have been able to tell that uncle of mine that I wanted to marry someone I loved, or to tell Alişan's uncle that I would eventually get my school certificate. Would I have refused to become a kuma, a second wife in a polygamous household if you hadn't entered my life...?"

"So, was it to Alişan's uncle that you were so adamant about getting a school certificate? Where did you get the certificate from?"

"You remember me telling you that I stayed with Alişan's uncle in Mersin while he was doing his national service, that's where I studied while helping with the housework. I managed to sit the exams and passed. It was just as well that your father had persuaded my grandfather to get me a birth certificate because they wouldn't issue a school certificate without it."

"Well done, Zelo, you're a very intelligent girl."

"I'm afraid intelligence isn't worth a dime if you haven't got luck to go with it."

"In my opinion, you stood in the way of your own luck. Imagine running off to elope with the caretaker's son. Do you realise they could have killed you for that?"

"One doesn't fear death when one is young. I had thought that it would be better to die young than to go to bed with someone I didn't love. As if dying was easy! We were lucky then, Nevo. We got away with it. Alişan was saved thanks to his national service and I was saved thanks to my grandfather."

"You can say that again."

"According to Alişan, the tribesmen did go looking for him at the barracks. Apparently, they spoke to his commanding officers who told them that it was absolutely impossible for him to hide his girlfriend there. They assured them that the girl they were looking for was not there and that they should be looking elsewhere for her. Thanks to that Alişan was saved by the skin of his teeth. As for me, thankfully my grandfather intervened and stopped the tribesmen searching for me."

"Really, how?"

"Well, I understand he threatened them saying that if they dealt with me according to their laws then he would leave all of his fields, vineyards and gardens to the nation. They would get nothing at all."

"I know he loved you very much but I didn't realise that he would go that far for you."

"But it seems that there was a reason for this, Nevo. Apparently, he had a particular soft spot for his first born son, my oldest uncle. My grandfather doted on him but, unfortunately, he fell in love with a girl from a neighbouring tribe. Her family was opposed to the relationship and refused to let them get together. So, he just kidnapped her. The girl's relatives tracked him down and shot him repeatedly in the head and chest. Those that saw his body said that his face was totally unrecognisable. My grandfather was inconsolable. He was in mourning for years. You may remember my telling you that my own father was the victim of such a vendetta. Cevahir Ana told me all this later and that's why he stopped them from killing us."

"What I'm dying to know, Zelo, is why you didn't think of contacting us way back then when you were in all that trouble?"

"Of course, I thought about it but how the hell was I to know where you were. I didn't have your address, remember? I told you that my mothers must have destroyed your letters fearing that you'd firstly encourage me to continue with my education and later, with the Alişan business, that your father might take me under his wing. You can't imagine how they pressurised me when they realised that Alişan and I were in love. Believe me they really gave me a rough ride then."

"So what happened next?"

"When Alişan finished his national service he came back for me at his uncle's house. From there we moved to Antalya. He got himself a job on a construction site as a brick layer. There was a lot of constructions of hotels going on in Antalya in those days. He managed to earn good money and was never out of work during the summer months. However, it wasn't so easy during the rainy season so he got himself a job as a guard on one of those sites. In fact we lived on one such site and didn't have to pay any rent. Then I got pregnant. We were so happy. I thought that if I had a baby it may be a way of reconciling with my family, my grandfather might act as a go-between and have us forgiven for the baby's sake. I missed my mothers, mostly my own mother Kader Ana of course. I longed to see her but my only hope was my grandfather. He was the one and only person who might achieve it. You remember how much I loved him?"

"He was very fond of you too! God rest his soul. So what about the baby?"

"There was no baby, I miscarried after six months. The baby was stillborn."

"Oh no! You poor darling."

"Apparently, there's no chance for a baby born that early. I nearly died too. I lost a lot of blood so I was confined to bed and took a long time to recover. The doctors insisted that I should stay in bed, just as they had done for your mother. They ordered me to stay in bed for at least four weeks. But you know me, I was up and about, cooking, cleaning and even scrubbing floors. I washed and ironed Alişan's clothes. My pains kept on returning because I wasn't looking after myself properly. Just as I thought I was getting better I started to bleed again. Eventually I had no alternative but to go back to the doctor. I was told that I would undergo another operation. Alişan didn't lay a hand on me for a long time. You know something, Nevo? I realised then that what Alişan really wanted was an entry into our clan through me. He thought that if we had a baby they might forgive us and take us back but when I miscarried that was the end of his hopes. I was simply a burden on him."

"I can't believe that. I'm sure he must have loved you."

"At first yes, but he didn't even marry me when I became of age."

"In other words, you never got married. Is that it?"

"How could we? I wasn't old enough... By the time I was eighteen, he was already in love with someone else."

"Oh, no! I can't believe this," I said angrily. "Not that, too!"

"There was a grocer near the construction site where we lived. Alişan fell in love with a young girl he kept bumping in-to while doing our shopping. As if that wasn't enough he also ended up having his wicked way with her. I had no idea that this was going on for months. I blamed myself thinking that I wasn't able to do my duty as a wife but I was also unhappy that he didn't even try with me. Little did I know that the bastard had already made sure he had an alternative."

I stretched my arms over the table and held her hand. Her eyes were tearful but she was not crying.

"How did you find out?"

"He told me himself."

"What!?"

"Yes, he said, 'You're unwell, there's a girl I know who could come and look after you and do the housework as well. I'm sure that you'll get well soon if you have a chance to rest.' Of course, I believed him at first. 'How much are we to pay her?' I asked. 'She doesn't want money as long as we feed her while she is staying with us.' 'What do you mean Alişan?' I asked him. 'Apparently, she doesn't have anywhere to live, so she will help us in return for bed and board,' he answered.

Zelha stopped for a moment and gulped.

"'Alişan, tell me frankly, have you found yourself another woman. Is that what you're trying to tell me,' I asked. 'You're not well, I think she can be useful to both of us until you get better,' he replied as if he were kidding a child."

"Is that why you left him?"

She sat staring at the wall opposite her as if she were watching an interesting film and did not speak for a while. Then she continued in her husky voice.

"Finally one day he brought her home. I pulled Alişan aside, 'Tell her to take her bundle and get out of here,' I told him. 'Otherwise, I'll go myself. I'll tell my mother how you've treated me and you'll soon have the whole tribe after you. My grandfather won't be able to stop them,' I threatened.

"Did she go?"

"No, apparently she was already carrying his baby."

We sat in silence again for a while. Her eyes were downcast as if she and not Alişan were to blame.

"When I tried to leave, he begged me to stay explaining that polygamous marriages were part of our tradition anyway. 'I've risked my life for you. I have turned my back on my tribe. Is this the way you repay me, Alişan?' I asked. He threw himself at my feet sobbing and begging me to stay. I suppose he was scared stiff that my family would come after him and the consequences that bore."

"Wasn't he at all embarrassed?"

"Not at all, it was all planned, Nevo. He tried to persuade me that he was concerned for my well being and that he was petrified that I would die if I miscarried again. For that reason he had not wanted me to get pregnant again. He reminded me of what I had been through before. 'And, just listen to this,' he went as far as to say that it was because I was the apple of his eye that he bought this kuma home so that she could give birth to our children and do the housework while I lounged around all day.

Zelha threw her cigarette on the floor and stamped on it. A long piece of ash had fallen on my skirt; I shook that on to the floor.

"Would you like another one?"

"Why not?"

I gave her another cigarette from the packet on the table. She took the lighter I had given her from her pocket and lit her cigarette. She took an enormous puff and blew the smoke from her lungs with all her strength.

"I tried to put up with the situation, because I didn't think I had an alternative. The next thing was that Alişan installed her on the mattress we used to share and I was relegated to the divan in the hallway. I was doing no housework at all and wasn't speaking to either of them. I spent days just looking out of the window, lounging on the divan knitting or simply sulking. At night, I would put my head under the pillow to stifle my sobbing so that they wouldn't hear me crying... At first they were careful not to be too lovey dovey in front of me but as time went by they lost all respect for me. Then, one night, I heard her moaning in his arms as they were making love. The pain was unbearable; it was like fire was flowing through my veins, Nevo. It was as if a ball of fire inside me gradually made its way to my groin and from there down my legs. It felt as if my body from the waist down was on fire. My heart, too, was on fire. I could hardly get myself out of the house. It was as though my body and soul were being ripped apart. I stayed outside in the frosty, night air until the morning. All my joints were stiff when I woke up. I was in bed for three or four days, the kuma girl looked after me but I didn't say a word. Neither to her nor to Alişan. Not a single word. I remained totally silent. One morning, when I finally got my strength back, I left the house after Alişan had gone to work and walked to the chemist to buy some aspirin. I returned home, put a mug of water by my bedside and started to take the aspirin one by one. I don't know how many I had taken when I suddenly remembered my grandmother's corpse. Her wrinkled face had turned a dirty yellow. They had tied up her jaw and had put a knife on her chest. Cevahir Ana had taken me to her bedside and made me kiss her veined hand. I was so petrified that I couldn't sleep for days. I was absolutely disgusted by the sight of her. Then I thought of Alişan seeing my corpse when he returned home. That's how he would remember me, laying there in my own excrement and with saliva all over my face. Who knows, maybe he would be pleased to be rid of me. When I thought of these things I dragged myself to the lavatory, shoved my fingers down my throat and started to vomit. The kuma came after me. I picked up my clogs from the floor and cursing her, threw them at her head. She ran away to the next room. Then I dragged myself back to bed and stayed there until the evening. I was still alive but my stomach was in a dreadful state. 'If I don't die by the morning I'll be alright,' I thought.

I felt so weak and eventually, I fell asleep. When I woke up the next morning, neither Alişan nor the girl were there. My head was spinning and I couldn't get myself out of bed. 'My God!' I thought, I didn't die yesterday but I am about to die now. I prayed to God, 'Please forgive me, God. At least let me go back to my village to die in my mother's arms. If I am to die let it not be like this, because of Alişan and the pills. Let my uncles and nephews take their revenge. If they kill me they will probably kill Alişan, too, which is just as well. Let him suffer the way I'm suffering for my sins.' I got out of bed and with great difficulty staggered from chair to table to get to the lavatory. On the way back, I became so weak, I only made it as far as my old matrimonial bed, the bed Alişan and the girl now used. I collapsed in a heap there and fell asleep. What I had feared happened while I was asleep, I vomitted again. Apparently when the two of them returned home and found me lying there, they decided not to touch me and instead they slept on my divan in the sitting room. I slept in the same bed the following night as well. I ate the yoghurt and drank the tea and soup that the girl gave me. I started feeling a bit better. Since God had spared me, I decided to return to my village. I waited for a few days to build up my strength and then one day, after Alişan had left, I got up and dressed. As I walked to the door, the girl asked me where I was going, I didn't answer her. I left without taking anything. Can you imagine? Nothing, no bundle, no bag, no nothing! I walked out of there just as I had walked out of the village and made straight for the bus-stop. I kept on changing buses until I reached my village at the end of the second day."

"You went back to the farm?"

"Yes, I went back to the farm. Where else could I go? Does a person who has put her life in danger fear a beating, scolding or humiliation?"

"What did they do when they saw you?"

"Nobody recognised me at the gate, because I was totally covered in black. You know there's quite a distance between the gate and the house. I walked very slowly, every step brought back different memories. Would you believe it if I told you that I even remembered how excited I was when my mother and I walked down that same path before going to meet your father for the first time, at his office. Then he sent us to your house. Anyway, to cut a long story short, when I got to the women's courtyard, I uncovered my head. The first one to recognise me was Halide. She screamed at the top of her voice. All the women surrounded me and started yelling. My mother; Kader Ana almost fainted. Cevahir Ana silenced everybody and she had the doors closed. Before saying anything to my uncles and the rest of the men, she sent word to my grandfather. Apparently he was unable to walk anymore and had changed a lot. They made me wear the black scarf over my head again and took me to him before anyone else could see me. He was the first one to hear what I had to say. It was as if I were giving evidence."

"I'm sure, he must have been very pleased to see you."

"He started to shake uncontrollably; I was scared that he might die, Nevo. He had become very old while I was away but maybe before when I saw him every day, I didn't notice him aging. The old man before me was now like a very old, stately oak tree. There were thick veins and liver spots all over his hands. The spark in his eyes had gone out. He was left with only two teeth in his mouth. He certainly had one foot in the grave. Worst of all was that the kind expression on his face was definitely gone. My grandfather's life was slipping away and he was waiting for the end. I threw myself at his feet praying God that I could give him some years of my life. He was trembling as I was crying. I didn't want to upset him so I didn't tell him why I had left Alişan. I simply said that I regretted my actions and missed my mothers, my family, my home and my village. I begged for forgiveness and kissed his hands over and over again. He agreed to take me under his wing just as he had always done. He had my bed made up on the floor in a room opposite his own in case anyone tried to harm me. I stayed with him until I married. My grandfather spoke to each of my uncles and nephews one by one and managed to persuade them to take me back. Of course, some of them gave me a hard time but it wasn't that bad, thanks to the respect and regard they had for my grandfather."

"Then what?"

"I told my mothers all about the miscarriage and my subsequent ill health. They fed me with fresh cream and honey every day and a concoction they made up of medicinal herbs. Finally, the colour returned to my cheeks and I was able to pull myself together. A few months after I got better, they chose a husband for me and that's all there is to it."

"But I remember they were very keen to give you as a bride to the Karançi tribe. Kader Ana was always talking about it."

"My God! You certainly have a good memory, Nevo."

"Not really. When we were in our second year at school my father gave me a diary which I had scribbled in. A few years ago when I was moving house, I found that diary in one of the chests. Immediately, I sat on the floor and read it from cover to cover. That's why I even know the name of the tribe."

"Would the Karançis accept a girl who had eloped with Alişan? I think not! It was just as well that I wasn't promised to one of them when I was still a child. Had that been the case they certainly wouldn't have let me live."

"Haven't you ever felt like killing Alişan yourself, Zelo?"

"Haven't I just! When he first brought that girl home, I kept on toying with the idea of bashing their heads in while they were asleep. But, I'm sure you'll agree if someone isn't evil inside, it's not possible to become a murderer, no matter how angry one is. As I just told you, I couldn't even bring myself to complain about him to my grandfather and uncles."

"I suppose you didn't want to cause trouble for your family either."

"No, not necessarily for that reason, Nevo. Do you remember Ado? Ado, the one we were all scared of... You know who I mean, the one Cevahir Ana caught as he was trying to hammer a nail into a cat's head. She gave him a good beating with a piece of wood..."

I winced when I remembered Hairy Ado. He was big for his age and had huge eyebrows.

"How can I forget him? We cried for days on end for that poor cat."

"Well, you see, Ado never changed a bit. He shot a few men and went to jail a few times, but was pardoned each time. One day after I had returned home, he came up to me in the garden. 'Zelo,' he said, 'tell me where that bastard you eloped with is, so that I can go and finish him off. It's obvious that he made you unhappy; let me give him a taste of his own medicine.' 'Leave me alone Abdullah,' I said. 'Don't you go causing any more trouble,' I warned. 'These things are child's play to me, just a game! In fact your uncle always makes me do his dirty work for him.' He said, 'All you have to do is tell me his name. I'll find him wherever he is and finish him off. Nobody needs to know.'

For a split second, I felt like giving him that treacherous Alişan's address but I couldn't. It must have been because I'd loved him so much and, in spite of all the pain he had caused me, there must have been a morsel of love left in my heart for him. What a shame that I've wasted all my love on the wrong man.

"But, what about your present husband? If he took you on knowing all about you and Alişan, he must really love you deeply. Isn't that so?"

"Yes, that's true. Şiyar never reproached me about that."

"But you weren't to blame Zelha. Maybe you just made a mistake because you were so young, we all make mistakes."

"All the same, anyone else may not have accepted it that easily. He might have thrown it back in my face every once in a while. Şiyar was a mature widower with children. His wife had died three years earlier. I was only nineteen and he was already forty. Of course I wasn't that keen on marrying him but with my past I didn't have the front to argue, Nevo. Being given to an elderly man wasn't such a big punishment when, after all, I was willing to pay for my sins with my life. Anyway that was how I felt when I went to the county town as his bride. It's just as well I did go. Şiyar both loved and respected me. He made his children respect me, too. He handled me with kid gloves. Within a year I got pregnant and Kader Ana came to stay with us. She made me stay in bed and took very good care of me and spoiled me. I was very scared that I would lose my baby again. Şiyar had promised to send me to the hospital when it was due and he kept his promise. Can you imagine woman? I gave birth to my baby in a hospital! Whoever heard of the likes of us having babies in a hospital? Most of my husband's relatives were angry that I hadn't had the baby at home with the help of a midwife but he wouldn't hear of it. We had a son and two years later I gave birth to our twins. So, you can see that until I got mixed up with all this business I was a normal housewife and mother. And very happy I was, too. But there you are, Şiyar's older sons were first to get involved. Inevitably their father was drawn into it, too. I warned him so many times, 'The boys are young, they're teenagers, don't poke your nose into these matters,' I said. But once one family member was involved the others were all pestered to join in, too. No one was let off the hook. If you decided to be neutral, you were automatically considered as an enemy by both sides. Being a Chief's grandchild and a popular, loved and respected person in the area they wouldn't leave him alone. You have to side either with the state or with the organisation, otherwise you'd be left out in the cold. Finally Şiyar was obliged to support his own people. In short, Nevo, the fickle finger of fate had it that just when I was beginning to feel comfortable, trouble started and my life was turned upside down again."

“Not only yours, my darling, many people’s lives were turned upside down.”

“You can say that again. It became impossible to live where we were. I felt very uneasy and kept on nagging my husband that we should move. That was when Şiyar went into politics. In actual fact his uncles had been in politics since the first Assembly was established. You may have heard of the famous Miroğulları family... Anyway, when my husband applied for his candidacy and got elected to parliament, we moved to Ankara. I wish, we hadn’t. Big deal! Look where it’s got us! Because we went to Ankara at my insistence, I had to carry the banner for Şiyar when he was taken into custody. I unexpectedly found myself involved in politics up to my ears. You know the rest…”

“My poor darling,” I said. “It seems that you weren’t elected to be an MP you were simply used as a scapegoat. If you hadn’t married, all these terrible things wouldn’t have happened to you. I wish you could have accomplished things that would benefit your region. If only you were able to sort out these problems one by one.”

She dropped her cigarette on the floor and stubbed it out with her foot.

“Don’t irritate me woman,” Zelha replied. “I came to the ball and now I must dance to their tune. *Inshallah*, in time my region will benefit from my efforts.”

“If only you hadn’t been implicated in these matters.”

Suddenly, a shadow passed across her face. It was very obvious that she hadn’t actually chosen to become involved. She was able to speak to me frankly, because, we had managed to recapture in such a short time that closeness we had established thirty-five years ago. She was able to open her heart to me but, needless to say, there are always limits. Suddenly, Zelha sat upright and leaned back in her chair.

"What you euphemistically refer to as 'these matters' is our cause, Nevo. It appears that God Almighty wants me to be involved in this cause. I could have been sent as a bride to the Karançis when I was fourteen and who knows by now I could have had nine or ten children. Or, I could have stayed on in Alişan's home and helped his kuma bring up their children all the while aching inside. I could even have stayed in Sarıcadan preparing pastries with my mothers. No matter how you look at it there was no way out for me. At least, now I am struggling honourably for my people." She leant forward and continued, "That's enough about me what about you? Are you married? Do you have any children?"

"I was married. I am divorced and I have a son."

"May God be with him. Why did you get divorced, Nevo? I sincerely hope that you didn't have to deal with a kuma, too, did you?"

I couldn't reply immediately. Strangely enough I didn't really know why I divorced my husband so how on earth was I going to explain it to her. I am sitting on my chair my hands clasped between my legs and my shoulders slumped forward, just like a guilty student sitting in front of her teacher. After listening to my story would my friend find me guilty? I don't have a single word in my own defence. Possibly, the guilt is mine. I am certainly guilty of being spoilt and extravagant. I'm spoilt, because, I haven't been able to appreciate the love that was bestowed on me. I'm extravagant, because

I have squandered away all the opportunities that were given to me. What can I say to this honourable woman sitting opposite me? We were both born in the same country but, I grew up with all the privileges that my poor friend couldn't even imagine and yet, I had no doubts in divorcing my husband simply, because I was bored. I am a woman who ended her marriage when she realised that she was falling in love with someone else. So, how can I, of all people, explain myself to this woman whose destiny was dictated by her tribe, this woman who had to give up the love of her life because she couldn't share him with a second wife.

"Was it you who asked for the divorce?" she asks.

I nod my head signalling yes.

"Why? Was he unfaithful to you?"

I was tempted to say yes and move on, but how could I lie to my blood sister? Hadn't we sworn ourselves to each other with that blunt nail when we were only nine years old?

"No."

"Did he physically abuse you?"

"No, never."

"So why then?"

"He left..."

"He left you because of another woman. Is that it?"

"I said no, didn't I? He left, because we didn't get on together."

I wonder, if Zelha whose only reason for divorce would be infidelity will believe me if I told her that he left because of a kitchen mixer? I have fooled myself by thinking it was that for years now but I have finally come to terms with the fact that it was me who left the marriage. Murat was not at fault at all and what's more, I now regret my actions. How can I tell my friend who has suffered even to the extent of imprisonment simply because she is a woman from Eastern Anatolia? I blush as those last twenty-four hours, which hurriedly brought about our divorce, flash before me like a film clip. My throat is dry and I am desperately trying to hold back the tears.

NEVRA

Apart from the plans, we had made to celebrate our tenth wedding anniversary in the evening, that rainy November Wednesday started out just like any other day. The alarm clock went off precisely at seven. Murat got up first, laid the table and prepared breakfast as usual. After I dozed for a while I got up, yawned and stretched before going to the lavatory. I then picked up the newspaper from outside the front door and made my way to the kitchen. As soon as I entered, I saw a huge package wrapped in shiny red paper set by my place at the table. A big grin spread across my face and I hesitantly asked what it was.

"Open it and you'll see," answered my husband.

There was nothing on the wrapping paper to indicate what may be inside. One thing was for sure, it was too big to be something romantic. It was obvious that there wouldn't be a piece of jewelery in it. I looked inquisitively at my husband who was nonchalantly sprinkling salt on his hard boiled egg.

"It's a big box but not big enough for a car, is it?" I said.

"No."

"So, what is it?"

"Something you've wanted for ages."

I closed my eyes trying to imagine what it could possibly be. He went to a lot of trouble getting it gift-wrapped. Was he trying to fool me? Was there a box within a box, within a box? Maybe a tiny diamond something… a flight ticket to India… the velvet jacket I had seen in the Armani window which I would have died for. They would be a big drain on our budget which would be hard for him to justify. But wasn't our tenth anniversary worth it? I looked at my husband intently trying to guess from his expression what it may be.

"Would you like me to pour you some tea?" he asked.

"Not yet, I'd better wake Cengiz or he'll be late for school."

"Aren't you going to open your present first?"

"Indeed I am!"

I wish I hadn't. But I did. I tore off the shiny red paper and cut the string around the cardboard box with a knife and removed my present with the care of a doctor delivering a baby. I held it firmly in both hands and placed it gently on the table. It was a food processor, a food processor; you could have knocked me down with a feather.

"Apparently it does twelve different jobs," said Murat proudly.

I busied myself around the kitchen trying to hide my utter disappointment, but when I could no longer suppress it I stood by the table opposite him and spoke, trying to soften my husky voice.

"Is this it? Is this what I get on our tenth anniversary?" I asked.

"Don't you like it?"

I didn't reply. Whenever I'm edgy, my voice becomes shrill, no matter how hard I try to control it.

"I thought you'd wanted one for quite some time now, Nevra?"

"A food mixer! Is that it?"

"How many times have I had to listen to your complaints about slicing onions or whipping eggs? What's more it does loads of tricks, for instance..."

"Please don't go on, I don't want to hear any more about it."

"But, Nevra..."

"No buts. Today is our tenth wedding anniversary. We got married ten years ago today."

"That's why I got you something that you wanted and something that would be useful too."

"Is there some sort of hidden agenda here? Are you insinuating that I've not been a good wife and mother? You may be right but don't forget that I've been working, too. I've never shown you up when we go out, I am always well turned out. I'm just the same as when you married me."

"When did I ever complain about any of this?"

"Never, but I'd rather you said something to my face than making sly insinuations."

"There's no such thing."

"In that case, it's even worse. You obviously have no understanding of the sensitivity of a woman. There's not one iota of romanticism in you. You don't know how to appeal to a woman's soul. What a shame"

"What the hell have I done to deserve this?"

"You've bought me a bloody food processor as a tenth anniversary present, that's what!"

"Is it worth getting this worked up over?"

"If you can't understand how I feel, I might as well throw myself out of the window," I shouted.

"Stop shouting at once. That's enough. I still don't understand what you're getting so worked up about."

"Oh really! You see no reason for my anger, eh Murat?"

"None whatsoever in my opinion."

"There's plenty in my opinion and I don't mind telling you... Is this what you consider a worthy present for me? Of all things, this!"

I hit the mixer, bang, bang, bang with my hand. I was aware that I was shrieking more and more and my face looked uglier the more I screamed. Murat's surprise gradually turned to anxiety.

"Nevra, for God's sake, keep it down! Cengiz'll hear you, not to mention the neighbours."

I felt worse realising that my husband cares more about what the neighbours think than how I feel. I screamed louder.

"Is this what I get for ten years with you? Is this it?"

"You know it's not only this. Haven't I invited our friends to the theatre and then to your favourite restaurant tonight too? Or doesn't that count?"

"Count? Count? God knows you must have jotted down every lira spent in your little notebook to count it up."

"Of course I did, Nevra. I'm no Croesus after all. Money doesn't grow on trees you know."

"I know that very well since you never stop telling me so, that's why I never ask you for anything. We go out once in a blue moon. It has to be a birthday or an anniversary before we can go anywhere nice. We haven't even had another child, because, you keep on reminding me that you're not Croesus."

"Correct me if I am wrong but wasn't it you who didn't want another child so why blame me and another thing, is it my fault that the restaurants have become so expensive. The prices have gone through the roof lately."

"Don't change the subject. We were arguing about this bloody present! The mixer you decided to buy me for my anniversary!"

"Let's leave it there... enough is enough..."

"A FOOD MIXER!" I shouted

"Look here; do you know how much I paid for this food mixer?"

"AN EXPENSIVE FOOD MIXER!"

When he can't stop me shouting, he stomps out of the kitchen slamming the door behind him. I collapsed on to the chair and started crying. It's only when Cengiz came in that I tried to pull myself together.

"Why didn't you wake me up me, Mum?" he asked. "I'll miss the school bus now. Where's my toast?"

"I'm sorry my love, I'm not feeling myself this morning. Ask your dad to get your breakfast."

"I can do it myself and he can give me a lift to school."

I left my son in the kitchen and went back to the bedroom and lied down on the bed. There seemed to be a lump stuck in my throat and my eyes were burning. How on earth did we come to this, I wondered, what I've done to deserve a food processor as a tenth anniversary present. Apart from the gold bracelet his mother gave me and the ring Murat put on my finger on our wedding day, I've had nothing from the Tuna family, have I? Has my husband ever come home with a bunch of flowers? Has he ever surprised me with a gift or even celebrated Valentine's Day? Have we ever been on holiday alone together? Come to think of it, have we ever been out for a tête-à-tête dinner. As far as everybody sees, Murat is an ideal husband. When my friends and I run down our husbands, Nazan always says, 'Count your blessings, dear. Murat hands over everything he earns to you and never asks you to account for it. My old man gives me nothing, I haven't a clue how much he earns. I even have to plead for a pair of stockings.'

Another friend at work would often say, 'Do you know what my husband says without the slightest bit of embarrassment? He says that since we're both earning money why don't I pay my own expenses?"

Sevim on the other hand would point out that I didn't know what a vagrant husband was like, "That's why you complain about such insignificant things, Nevra. If you were me you wouldn't even think about the lack of presents. Believe me, if a man comes home bearing gifts, he's only trying to ease his conscience about the ding-dong he's having on the side. I swear to God, I'd rather not receive his gifts and sleep peacefully not wondering what he's up to again."

Because I had never had any such problems I looked at Sevim's fragile state in amazement. No, I must admit, never anything like that occurred. Murat was a loving husband and father. We've never had any ups, therefore we couldn't have any downs. No arguments, so, no reconciliations. Neither excitement nor pain, but I hasten to add that there hasn't been much bliss either. We just plodded along monotonously side by side. The only thing that has added a bit of colour to my life has happened since I began to work as a public relation officer for an advertising agency and I have always loved the job. Even though, it wasn't necessary for me to go to the office every day, I was happy to go three or four days a week, because I was bored to death by the quiet and order of our home. It made me feel as if I had died and gone to heaven before my time was up. I totally changed the minute I entered the hustle and bustle of the office. Gradually, over the four years I had been working, my peaceful paradise at home became purgatory for me.

Suddenly from my bed, I heard the front door closing and the sound of foot-steps down the stairs. I got out of bed and looked out of the window. Father and son were walking as one toward our car parked in the back yard. My son was carrying his bag full of thick books and my husband was carrying the burden of his difficult marriage on his shoulders. Both of them were walking with slumped shoulders weighed down by their heavy loads.

I wondered if I went too far. Was it worth making such a fuss over his present? I returned to the kitchen and fiddled with the bloody mixer. According to the instruction booklet it does twelve different things. Apparently it cuts, whips, slices and, and, and... Angrily I threw the booklet on the table. I was tired; I was at the end of my wits. I decided not to go to work but to go back to bed. Oh, what an excellent healer sleep was. It cuts out both good and bad things just as curtains cut out the light.

The shrill sound of the telephone ringing woke me up.

"What time are we meeting this evening?" asked Nazan

"Seven-thirty in front of the theatre."

"Your voice sounds strange. Are you OK?"

"Yes, I overslept."

"You never sleep this late, is anything wrong my pet? Everybody's going down with this flu bug. Please don't feel embarrassed if you think you should cancel this evening."

"No, for God's sake, Nazan. It's just that we went to bed late last night. I'll be as right as rain in no time."

"Who's a naughty girl then? You celebrated you anniversary a bit early didn't you?"

"Don't be ridiculous!"

"Wow! Not only are you sleepy you're also a bit snappy."

"You're right, I am a bit concerned."

"Don't tell me you're still worried about that Holland business. I thought that was all done and dusted."

"It is. We're not going."

"Frankly, I thought that it was an opportunity not to be missed but I'm sure you know best."

"Murat hasn't notified Holland of his final decision yet but we're not going. There's no chance of me getting a job there and we have to consider Cengiz's education. It's not easy moving to a new country or getting used to a new school."

"I don't necessarily agree. Children get used to new surroundings very easily. I bet you he'd get used to a new school within a month. As for you, you could always go to a language school to avoid getting bored."

"It's not that easy after a certain age."

"There is the internet you know, everybody uses it nowadays to keep in touch with friends all the time. Distance is no problem, but I don't want to go on about it, it's your decision however I'd think about it again if I were you"

"Nazan, we're not you. We've thought about it long enough and we've made up our minds. And don't you dare bring this up tonight," I said angrily.

"Of course not, I understand."

"OK. We'll see you this evening then."

"Just a sec. One more thing. Don't drive, take a taxi and save yourselves the aggravation of finding a parking space, we'll drop you back home afterwards."

I put down the phone feeling a little anxious. What if Murat cancels our plans or decides not to show up because he's angry with me? The husband I know would never do such a thing, but under these circumstances, I'd better call him and double check. I reluctantly dialed his office number. I hate giving in and being the one to make the first move when we've had an argument. Thank God, just as I had expected, his secretary Esma Hanım answers.

"Good morning, Esma Hanım, how are you today?" I asked.

"I'm fine, thank you Nevra Hanım, I hope all is well with you."

"I'd like you to give my husband a message please."

"Let me put you through..."

"No, no, there's no need for that. Just remind him that we're meeting our friends at the theatre this evening. I overslept this morning, maybe I'm getting the flu, so I wasn't able to speak to him before he left. I just want to make sure that he hasn't forgotten."

"I hope you feel better soon. Don't you worry I'll pass on the message immediately. Does Murat Bey know which theatre?"

"Yes, of course he does. Tell him to come straight there."

"Right away, Nevra Hanım. Oh, by the way, may I offer you my congratulations?"

"For?"

"I mean… your…"

"Of course, yes, thank you. How did you know?"

"A little bird told me."

"A bubbly little bird I bet," I remarked and Esma Hanım giggled.

"Enjoy your special day. I'll pass on the message.

I put the receiver down and went back to bed. I tried to imagine how different my life would have been if I had been Ferdi's wife instead of Murat's. Ferdi was one of the managers in the company I worked for. He was handsome and very sophisticated. I have been aware of the attention he pays me for quite some time now. He was always finding some excuse to talk to me, praise my work and even send messages on my computer. I wondered what it was that he liked about me. I was surprised that I could attract any man's attention in my dreary state. I must admit that as the excitement of my relationship with Murat wore off and monotony set in, my appearance deteriorated, too. Even my mother, who took particular care not to upset me, had started to comment on my weight and on what I ate. I couldn't bring myself to tell her that the weight had nothing to do with eating, drinking was the problem. She had no idea that I had developed the taste for a large gin and tonic every evening. For quite some time, I had been collapsing on the sofa in front of the television with my drink to watch the seven o'clock news. Murat wouldn't be home by then and I took the opportunity to grab a moment of happiness at the end of the working day with my lovely G and T relaxing on my own. That drink would give me the energy to cope with the monotony of family life; be it listening to my son's school news, which didn't interest me very much, or my husband's gossip about the bank. It soothed my nerves and calmed me down. The interesting thing, however, was that as soon as I was aware of Ferdi's attention, I gave up the gin and tonic so as to lose weight. I had cut my hair short and had it highlighted. I had taken advantage of the sales and bought a new jacket, a pair of boots and two blouses. I had even started to use pearlized lipstick and matching nail varnish.

"How lovely you look," my mother had said when we met for our usual fortnightly lunch. "Never let yourself go, my dear, a woman should always take good care of herself. Beauty is not enough!"

Funnily enough, I agreed with my mother that day having hated her for a long time. She had married a much wealthier man than my father who could provide her with all the luxuries of life, hairdressers, clothes, make-up etcetera. In fact, there had been a time when I couldn't even bear to look at her. I had vowed that I would never be like my mother. I wasn't going to be one of those tarted-up women with nothing other than their looks to offer their husbands. I would have an opinion, ideals and a career and to that end, I was determined to graduate from university then, if I should marry, he would first of all be my friend then my lover and finally my husband. How naïve I was. It was the same naivety as the women of Sarıcadam who knew nothing of the world beyond their garden gates. Listen to me, back to Sarıcadam again. Why can't I tear myself away from there? It must be because they were the most beautiful days of my life and it also happens to be when my character was at its best.

After we left Sarıcadam we lived in Ankara for a few months before my father was posted to various places on the Black Sea coast, to the East and finally to a town on the Aegean Coast. My brother was born while we were in Ankara, my parents were so happy to have had a son. The arrival of the fourth member of our family made us all very happy but those days of happiness were not to last long. A few years later, my father was again posted to the East and by this time there was no trace of happiness left in our family. My mother had turned into a sad, difficult woman. It had become clear to her that my father would never achieve her expectations for life. My brother wasn't old enough to understand what was going on around him, but day by day, I was becoming more and more frayed as a consequence of my parents' continuous quarrels. Even though, they made sure to have their arguments behind closed doors, I was still able to hear everything that was said.

"Not only have we been continuously posted to the primitive outposts of Eastern Anatolia, it seems that you have also put paid to the possibility of ever becoming a senior governor! I'm sick and tired of your foolish behaviour! Who the hell cares about those people out there? What business is it of yours whether they are treated fairly or not? What good will they do you? Maybe it's because you're one of them yourself. Are you? Answer me! Are you one of them eh? Are you?"

At times like that I used to run and lock myself in my room as if that would shut out the sound of their voices. While my mother would harp on at my father, I couldn't understand why he didn't have a go at her selfishness and extravagances. She was a woman who cared for nothing but her luxuries.

"You have no sense of justice at all, you haven't a glimmer of humanity in your heart, what sort of woman are you?" he would shout at the top of his voice.

With time their rows spread out of their bedroom into every corner of the house, most of all to the dinner table. There was no escape, it was impossible not to hear them by blocking my ears or burying my head under my pillows. Not only could I hear how unhappy they were but it was plain to see, too.

"Why do you always have to think of others? Don't you have a family? Shouldn't you be considering us as well? You have children to think of and what about me?"

"Me... me... me, always me! Of course, the world revolves around you doesn't it? You are the most important thing on this earth. Everything has got to be the way it suits you, the way you want it! We all have to think of you first and foremost."

"You're being very unfair. I'm not thinking of myself, I'm thinking of you."

"Me, pray tell me what exactly you're thinking about me, Nermin?"

"All of your colleagues have been appointed as governor generals here and there. Had you not been so stubborn you would have been appointed as the governor general of İstanbul or İzmir yourself by now. Can't you see it? Can't you see how stubborn you've been? My God, how stupid I've been to have chosen you as a husband. What a mistake that was! Can't you understand that you can't oppose the government all the time? Is it up to you to keep on arguing with them and criticising their policies? If you are so keen on preaching politics, why don't you join a political party? You might then become an MP, at least."

"Preaching politics, who's preaching politics? Don't poke your nose into things that you know nothing about. Differentiating between what's right and what's wrong doesn't necessarily mean criticizing their policies. A government official has to be just and fair."

"It's precisely because you're just and fair that we have been sent crawling in misery around Anatolia."

"Isn't Anatolia part of our homeland then?"

"Indeed, it is, but haven't we had our share of duty in these miserable places. If we are to be stuck out here, it would have been nice if you were appointed as the governor General instead of district governor. At least then I would have been able to enjoy the privileges of being your wife and no more arse-licking to all those governor General's wives as I've done throughout the years."

"You are under no obligation to do any of that. Have I ever crawled to any one of them? No!"

"It's exactly because you don't that I have taken it upon myself to do it for you. For your own good. For your future."

"Don't bother, Nermin, they're not going to promote me to a higher governorship that's for sure."

"How can you be so sure? How can say this to me so easily?"

"Because I am at ease with myself, that's why. I don't care about titles; I simply want to carry out my duties fairly."

"But I care. I haven't married you to shuffle from town to town. A person ought to have some ambition you know. What happened to that young man with a brilliant future ahead of him that I married? Tell me, I'm dying to know what happened to him?"

They divorced during my second year at the Lycee.

My mother was a beautiful woman and as soon as she divorced, my father she got married to a very wealthy landowner – an Ağa from Söke and they settled in İstanbul. My brother Orhan lived with my mother while I stayed on with my father since it was decided that it would not be wise for me to change schools. I reconciled with her while I was at university. She showered me with gifts and money so that I would forgive her. It was her idea that we should have tea somewhere near the university once a week and later, when I got married, she insisted that we meet up for lunch once a fortnight. She always wanted to meet at a shopping mall. We would dine at one of the many bistros and later go shopping when she would buy me gifts like blouses, skirts or shoes from the fashionable shops there. I think I'm right in saying that she was continuously trying to win back my love for her with these gifts. When we were together I often felt like stretching my hand and ruffling her lacquered hair or smudging her immaculate make-up to turn her into a normal human being, warm and natural. In retrospect, however, I suppose it was me who needed to relax and behave normally.

I pulled up my blanket and snuggled up to my pillow to go back to sleep, a deep sleep that might act as a miraculous cure for my wounded soul. If I could manage to sleep, I might have forgotten everything; this morning's fiasco, the shame of being a conservative suburban daughter of divorced parents, the feeling of being cooped-up in the windowless cell of my marriage, the monotony of my life and even how Ferdi makes my heart leap when he looks at me.

My sleep was interrupted yet again by the doorbell. I slipped on my dressing gown and run barefooted to the door. Standing by the door was the florist's delivery boy holding long-stemmed roses, probably ordered by Esma Hanım for Murat. Damn it, now I've got to find some change for a tip. Where the hell do I find change in this house? Was there no peace for the wicked!

After getting rid of the delivery boy I was looking at the card attached to the bouquet. It was a small simple card with the name Murat Tuna written in capital letters by the florist. Murat has obviously not found it necessary to add anything else to it. Neither an apology nor and appropriate endearment for such an occasion. Anyway how can one add a warm term of endearment when flowers are ordered over the phone? Whether I want to or not, I immediately made a comparison. Had they been from Ferdi, there would have been a little love poem on the card, that's for sure!

At quarter past seven I was standing in front of the theatre oblivious of the drizzling rain. Nazan was the first to arrive. We kiss each other twice without our lips touching our cheeks; the way the ladies who lunch do.

“Are you OK? Did you recover from your late night?” Nazan asked reproachfully.

“I was feeling a bit dopey this morning, that’s all. I hope I haven’t said anything to...”

“No, my darling, you said nothing wrong. I shouldn’t have commented on other peoples decisions, after all it’s your life isn’t it?”

“Please don’t say that. Surely we’re not other people, are we?”

“Of course not, that’s why I took it upon myself to speak the way I did. It’s because you had shared your anxieties with us and asked us whether it was a good idea to go or not that made me voice my opinion. That’s all; otherwise it’s none of my business.”

“Come on, don’t go on about it.”

Burhan came scurrying through the rain towards us.

“Wow, what dreadful weather! Was it raining like this when you got married ten years ago?”

“Indeed it was. I remember people saying that it’s supposed to be a blessing.”

“Well, you can’t say your marriage hasn’t been blessed, can you? There must be some truth in those old wives’ tales,” says Burhan. “So, where’s your hubby?”

“I’ll bet he’s stuck in a traffic jam,” I replied in a sheepish voice. “Traffic’s always bad when it rains.”

I felt rather edgy. What if he doesn’t come? Wasn’t I screaming at the top of my voice this morning? Didn’t I slam the door when I went to my bedroom? We didn’t speak after that but Esma Hanım must have given him my message. This evening was planned days ago. We had agreed that we would invite Nazan and Burhan to the theatre and then to the latest ‘in’ restaurant in Sıraselviler. After all is said and done that husband of mine was civilised enough not to spoil such an evening no matter how angry he was with me.

"Look, isn't that him?" said Nazan pointing to a man with his raincoat pulled over his head.

My heart sank when I looked at the man.

"No, that's definitely not Murat, he wouldn't hold his raincoat over his head like that," said Burhan.

"Let's move inside out of this drizzle," I suggested.

While we were queuing up to get inside, Murat arrived holding up his big black umbrella.

"I'm terribly sorry, you're soaking wet because of me. There's an awful traffic jam," he said apologetically. I tried to kiss him but his umbrella was in the way.

When we got inside and he folded his umbrella, he did not attempt to return my kiss. We don't even look each other in the eye. Nazan and I waited by the stairs while the men left their coats in the cloakroom.

We then proceeded to our seats upstairs and sit down.

"Thank you for the roses," I whispered in Murat's ear. He just smiled which meant that he was still angry with me.

After the play we walked to the restaurant. It has stopped raining but it was still damp underfoot. Nazan and I were walking arm in arm in front with our husbands following a few steps behind. When we reached the restaurant, we waited for them to catch us up before entering all together. The place was dimly lit.

"Would you care for a drink at the bar?" asked a waiter.

"No, thank you, we were at the theatre, it's already late," said Murat.

With that we were ushered to our table. Burhan chose the wine. Why? Wasn't Murat supposed to be doing that since we were the hosts? But that was Murat, always passive even leaving the choice of wine to a guest. He didn't like offending anyone and hates arguments. He's been always easy to get on with. I was trying to catch his eye to signal to him that he should choose the wine but I failed. I was obvious that we wouldn't be looking in to each other's eyes this evening. A short while later we were sipping our wine which had been served in huge glasses. Wow, wasn't the red wine good!

"Have you chosen what you are eating folks?" asked Murat. "I can recommend the steaks here, they're excellent."

Within an hour we have finished our dinner and polished off two bottles of wine. There was no trace of tension between Murat and I, we were relaxed and cheerful and a bit light-headed. We were surrounded by the buzz and music of the restaurant so we were speaking with raised voices and laughing continuously. We are all a bit tipsy.

Nazan raised her glass, God knows for the umpteenth time, "Here's to another ten years," she said.

"How can one put up with such a man for another ten years?" I asked. "He doesn't even know how to fight with a person properly."

"I suppose that a real man should be able to both love and beat his wife, isn't that so?" asked Burhan.

"One can't say she's had her fair share of beatings," Murat says downing the wine in his glass in one gulp.

"In that case, Murat, you should give her a real beating when you get home," said Nazan, "as a tenth anniversary present."

"I've already had my present," I said falling about laughing.

"Don't tell me it's the brooch you're wearing," said Nazan enviously.

"What a pity I couldn't wear my present this evening, it's a bit too big," I replied.

"What do you mean 'too big'; did he buy you a big present?"

"Yes, big, very big."

"Don't tell me he bought you a car."

"It starts with an 'M'. It's amazing, it's unbelievable."

"Come on then, out with it, I'm dying to know."

"You've got to guess."

"Give me a clue."

"I already did. It starts with an 'M'."

Nazan was thinking for a while gazing at the ceiling then she suddenly screamed, "A Mercedes."

"I can't believe it," said Burhan unable to conceal the jealousy in his voice. "You bought her a Mercedes at a time when nobody's job is safe. Have they given you a fat bonus or are you discretely emptying the bank's vaults?"

"You'd better pop in tomorrow and I'll show you my present if you promise not to be jealous," I said to Nazan.

"Unfortunately I haven't been able to buy my wife a Mercedes," said Murat shouting to make sure that he is heard. "Needless to say, nothing would give me greater pleasure but unfortunately, as you well know, I can't afford it." He was looking daggers at me but I was still laughing.

In my drunken stupor, I blurt out, "Here's to the 'M' waiting for me back home." My knees were wobbly and my head was spinning.

"Frankly Murat, I don't understand you. You're continuously complaining about your financial situation and yet, from what I hear, you've turned down an offer to work in Amsterdam. If you'd taken that job you could have bought cars for both your wife and your son," said Burhan.

"You've hit the nail on the head. Our son is not old enough to drive a car yet and that's exactly why we are not going."

We were all laughing again. For some unknown reason I seem to find everything funny. Maybe, I was trying to suppress the fact that I really wanted to cry. I was not telling Nazan what my present was in spite of her persistent questioning. When she got nothing out of me, she tried to find out from Murat.

"A mixer," said Murat very calmly.

"What do you mean a mixer?"

"A food mixer, it's just a food mixer."

"So what's so special about that?"

"It has twelve different functions, my dear," I interjected.

"Including giving you one?" Burhan asked making a rude gesture.

"Who's a naughty boy then?" I said laughing and accidentally spray wine from my mouth. Murat looked angrily at me again.

"If it does then I'd better get one too," said Nazan.

"Why, do we have a problem in that department?" asked Burhan.

"You should know the answer to that one," replied his wife.

As the conversation progressed, the tension between the four of us increased. While, at first, the effect of the wine had made us feel merry and slightly tipsy now, we were beginning to feel tense and susceptible. By the time the desserts arrive at the table, the atmosphere was very icy. Murat asked for the bill and we were all quiet and eager to leave this dark, noisy place as soon as the bill is settled.

Burhan and Nazan gave us a lift home as planned. Nobody said a word. Nazan, who was sitting in the front, had apparently passed out and had her head resting against the window. She was totally unaware of us getting out of the car.

"Thank you for a most wonderful evening," said Burhan before putting his foot down on the accelerator and speeding off. I waved at the departing car.

"Get a move on," said Murat in a firm voice.

He opened the main door and let me in. When I saw myself in the lift mirror, I turned my back on my husband. My make-up was smudged all across my face, there were black circles under my eyes and my hair was plastered to my head because of the damp air. I could feel the cream I had with the dessert churning in my stomach. As soon as were in our flat I rushed straight to the kitchen for a glass of water. Murat followed me, all the colour had drained from his face.

"Was it necessary for you to discuss my present with them?" he asked.

"Why shouldn't I?"

"You made a fool of me."

"If that's the way you felt why did you buy me a mixer in the first place?"

"For God's sake, how many more times do I have to tell you? You kept on saying that you'd like one so I thought it would please you. What's more I had to have it especially ordered as they didn't have one in stock."

"You'd better give it to your dear mother, she loves making cakes for you."

"Nevra, you've gone too far now. What the hell is the matter with you? What's your problem?"

"You're my problem."

"Why's that? Am I doing something wrong? Am I not always doing my best for you? Didn't I even turn down that Amsterdam offer because you didn't want to leave your job? What more do you want from me, Nevra? Tell me, what's our problem?"

"I don't know exactly how to put it... it seems to me that there's something missing in our relationship... it's just not working. You're not the right man for me."

"Because I bought you a mixer, eh?"

"No, because you don't seem to understand me... because you don't even try to. There's no excitement whatsoever in our life. There's no fun. I'm fed up, I'm bored to death. Can you understand that, Murat? I'm absolutely fed up."

"Sit down," he ordered pulling me roughly by the arm and making me sit down at the kitchen table. He sat opposite me.

"Is there someone else, Nevra?"

"What?"

"You heard, tell me the truth. Surely you know that I am a civilised man. If there is someone else, all you have to do is tell me and we'll do whatever is necessary. There's no need for screaming and shouting, no need to look for excuses like the mixer for instance..."

I jumped out of my seat and dash towards the work surface where the mixer is standing.

I opened the window and threw the mixer out shouting, "To hell with this bloody thing!" I heard it crash with a thump an instant later. Who knows where it landed, I was too scared to look out of the window. By the time I've closed the window, Murat has left the kitchen. I took a jug from the fridge and poured myself a glass of water. I collapsed on to the chair and gulped down the water as if I was drinking whiskey but I still could not calm down. I felt like breaking every single thing in the kitchen. I started to cry and my hands were shaking. I was waiting for Murat to come back and ask me why I was crying… why I was still in the kitchen… why I was not in bed… but he didn't. As time goes by I started to feel cold and so, a little while later, I went to the bedroom. My husband was not there. He's taken his pillow to who knows where. He couldn't be in the spare bedroom because Fatma Hanım who came to stay with Cengiz while we were out was sleeping there. I tip-toed to the sitting room door and peeped inside, Murat was on the sofa. I returned to the bedroom and slipped under the cold sheet shivering. I shut my eyes tightly in order to fall asleep and wiped out the dreadful events of this evening.

I woke up at the crack of dawn with my husband turning on the light; he was standing by the bed clutching his pillow and blanket. I sat upright in bed.

"Oh, you're awake," he said.

"You've woken me up. What time is it?" I looked at the clock on my bedside table. "It's not even seven yet."

"I got up before Fatma Hanım wakes up. I didn't want her to see that I'd slept in the sitting room."

"You shouldn't have slept there anyway."

"I have things to tell you."

"At this hour?"

"Yes," my husband come closer and looked me straight in the eye. "Listen Nevra, they're expecting a final answer regarding Holland today. I've changed my mind since last night and I'm going to tell them that I'll accept the job."

I couldn't believe my ears.

"You know that I don't want to go to Holland. I can't change my life-style at this stage and there's also Cengiz's schooling..."

"I'm not suggesting that you change anything, you do just as you wish but I'm going!"

"But that's not what we'd decided..."

"That was before last night."

"Are you telling me that our marriage is so weak that it won't even survive an argument over a mixer?"

"The issue here is not the argument, Nevra, it's your attitude. I didn't sleep a wink last night. I was weighing up all the pros and cons. You're not happy and therefore I'm not happy either. It was you who wanted to change certain aspects of our life not I. Maybe you're right, maybe it's about time we did. I've made up my mind, I'm going. It's up to you whether you come or not. Maybe a change of location might be good for our marriage."

"I wish you'd slept through last night instead of lying awake chewing over these things and coming to such silly conclusions. I can't live anywhere but Istanbul."

"If that's your decision then we'd better live apart for a while," said Murat.

I felt as if I've been kicked by a donkey and offered no response; I simply got out of bed and went to the kitchen. I stood by the window and looked at what I could see of the sky through the surrounding blocks of flats. The sky was tinged red as the sun rises. I open the window and leaned out, yes it was right there; the mixer has landed on the little blue car belonging to that education officer lady who lives at number five. It was broken in two, just like my marriage.

I didn't know how to explain all this to Zelha. She's looking straight at me with those dark penetrating eyes; ready and waiting to share my grief.

"We just didn't get along, that's all. He got a business offer from Holland that he couldn't refuse and I didn't want to leave İstanbul. He left and I stayed, it's as simple as that."

"Why didn't you go with your husband, Nevo?"

"I was happy with my job. I wouldn't be able to work there; it's very difficult for us to get work permits abroad nowadays."

"So, you were happy with your job but not with your husband. Tell me the truth, don't feel embarrassed. Was he treating you badly, did he beat you or something?"

"No, of course not."

"Was he jealous or possessive for instance?"

Obviously Zelha was not going to let me off the hook, so I resorted to a lie she unknowingly suggested to me.

"I felt suffocated and bored."

I felt comfortable with the lie even though Murat wasn't jealous or possessive at all, but at least the bored bit of it is true. I can't help thinking, however, that things might have been different had he been at least a bit jealous. He had always been understanding when I started working at the advertising agency. Sometimes I joined my colleagues for a drink after work and there were the official dinners that went on quite late but he never complained. He hadn't even noticed that during the latter part of our relationship, I had begun to take particular care of myself. I lost weight, changed my hair style and colour and spent a considerable amount of money on new clothes. I don't know if the end would have been any different though, even if he had noticed any of these changes and bothered to think about it a bit.

"How did your son react to the separation?"

"Well, of course, he was very unhappy about it but then my son is very mature for his age. He didn't blame either of us."

"I assume, he stayed with you."

I got hot flushes and started to blush. Apart from appearing in my friend's eyes to be an incapable woman who hasn't been able to make a go of her marriage, now, I was also going to appear as a bad mother too. I took a deep breath before saying anything.

"He's with his father."

"Really!"

I could detect the surprise and disappointment in her voice.

"We didn't want Cengiz to go through the rigmarole of those useless exams at the end of his primary school. We thought that it would be better for him to get a good education and learn a foreign language abroad... I mean for his own good... Don't forget I was working at the time and wouldn't have had enough time to devote to him, you see..."

"Did you say his name's Cengiz?"

"Yes, Cengiz."

"Your father must have chosen his name."

"Yes, how did you know?"

"Well, you remember your brother who died..."

I couldn't understand what she was on about, "Orhan… my brother hasn't died. He's perfectly well, touch wood. God bless him."

"No, for God's sake, I don't mean Orhan I mean the baby your mother lost when you were still in Sarıcadam…"

"What about it?"

"It's just that your father had named that poor baby Cengiz."

"How did you know that, Zelha?"

"I just do," replied Zelha. "There are certain things in life one never forgets. It's incredible how fresh my childhood memories are in my mind."

"Likewise, but how did you know what my father intended to call his son?"

"Your father had come to have lunch with my grandfather at the big house on the farm; you must remember the *selamlık* section of that house, Nevo. It was on the left as you entered the farm. They had had a long chat alone together in the room with all the divans. I remember it so well. One of my mothers had given me a tray with two cups of ayran to take to them."

"So…?"

"So, then, after your father had left, I heard my grandfather telling my uncle, 'Consider it done, apparently our district officer had intended to call his son Cengiz, too. He promised to do everything he can in the memory of his son!' So there you are I never forgot that."

"You're incredible even I didn't know that. So, who was the other Cengiz then?"

"My uncle's son, my cousin. I got the impression that my grandfather had asked your father to help that particular cousin in some way."

"I'm amazed, you know so much, Zelha."

"I certainly do, but remember we children were always running around under everyone's feet. We were in and out all the time, so, we knew everything that was going on. In fact I had heard that my mother was going to be sent to your house before she was told."

"Really?"

"Yes, I didn't miss a thing. I heard my grandfather speaking to Cevahir Ana saying, 'Our district officer's wife is unwell. They need someone to help out in the house. It can't be just anyone. Let's send Kader, she speaks a bit of Turkish and has also had midwifery experience. If it proves necessary, she may also be able to help the lady in that department, too. I remember running straight to my mother and telling her. I had cried floods of tears all day complaining that I didn't want to be separated from her. There was no consoling me even though she said that Cevahir Ana and auntie Satı would look after me well. All the same, I raised hell. Then, she came up with a solution. She persuaded my grandfather that since the lady of the house had a daughter of my age, it might be a good idea if she took me with her. I could keep you busy playing together."

"Thank God, she did," I said most sincerely. "Believe me Zelha; I've never in my life had another friend like you."

Zelha reached across the table and took hold of my hand affectionately.

"So, in other words you let your son go with your husband?" she asked disapprovingly.

"Well, he stayed with me at first while Murat sorted things out in Amsterdam and settled in. In the meantime, I changed my job about a year after Murat left. I became a journalist which involved working long days and late nights and I worried for my son. It was then that I decided he should be with his father. He's going to a very good school there and learning three languages at the same time. We spend our summer holidays together and I go over to visit him at every opportunity."

"How old is he now?"

"He was ten when we separated, so he'll be fifteen soon. He's a young man now at an age when he needs a father more than a mother. He gets on very well with his father. Murat is a kind and sensitive man who dotes on his son."

"But don't you miss him?"

"Don't I just. At first it was so unbearable that I even considered having Murat send him back, but Cengiz was happy there and preferred to stay in Amsterdam. If he had come back there would be no one at home when he got back from school and he'd be spending hours going to and from school through the Istanbul traffic jams. As it is now, he goes to his sports club after school, he plays tennis, swims and spends time with people of his own age. Apparently, his father picks him up on the way home from work. He's never lonely, has no problems with the traffic and doesn't have to worry about anarchy. Amsterdam is a quaint civilised city."

"Have you actually divorced now?"

"Eventually, we did."

"So, why's your surname still Tuna?"

"Because, Tuna not only sounds good but it also suits my articles. It's short and concise. I have never liked surnames ending with 'son' tying us to a family. As long as Murat doesn't mind I, intend to keep it this way."

"Hasn't he married again?"

"No."

"Maybe he's still waiting for you to change your mind, Nevo."

"I don't think so actually," I replied.

"And what about you? Have you been on your own ever since the divorce?"

"Not really."

"So there is someone. Out with it, who's the man in your life now. Come on, I'm dying to know."

"There's no one right now Zelo. I split up from him too almost two years ago now."

"Why?"

"It's difficult to explain."

"Nonsense! Do tell me, after all I've told you all about myself. Aren't we still blood sisters?"

Looking at Zeliha's dark eyes gazing at me made me feel like putting my arms around her, burying my head in her chest and while crying my eyes out, tell her the things I've never told anyone else. I knew she was that special friend who would neither judge nor question me in any way. I felt completely at ease with her and was so happy to be together again withed my soul mate. I wished it were possible for my tears to soothe the pain seared in my heart and to rid me of my regrets. I wished my friend and I could be running hand in hand breathlessly through the Sarıcadam countryside... I wished we could go down to the stream again, take of our shoes and stockings and paddle in the water getting our clothes wet. My only worry back then was that my mother would tell me off... like when I used to pick broom and daisies from the hillside and bundle them up in my skirt... like when we used to roll over and over in the grass, first me on top and then Zelha, as if one body and soul just as we were back then. I'd love to open up and disclose what's in my heart and share everything with her yet again…

I could hardly utter a word but finally came out with, "He's married, Zelo."

We both remained silent for a while, eventually she said, "Don't wreck the home of another woman. Please don't; find yourself another man."

"It's all in the past anyway."

"Did he go back to his wife?"

"I don't really know, I suppose so."

"Was it you who left him?"

"Yes."

"Believe me you're better off this way, Nevo. Much better off. The world is full of men, for God's sake find yourself a single man or you'll never be rid of problems. You'll go through the same ordeal over and over again."

"Is this the voice of experience? Did you fall for a married man, too?"

"No, my darling, I didn't. Thank God he spared me that ordeal. But I know only too well what it is like to share your husband with another wife, a kuma. My mothers, grandmothers and aunts all know that feeling very well. Don't you kid yourself that they liked the set-up but what else could they do, they have no choice in the matter. Even if outwardly they get on with their fellow wives there is always a fire burning inside. I can assure you that when they are trying to sleep in their beds, the jealousy and pain are unbearable. They want to die when they think of what's going on under the covers in the room next door. They lurk like foxes listening to the heavy breathing while they are burning inside. At daybreak, when they are together again, they laugh and joke but they can't wait to run each other down. Believe me, Nevo; it's very hard to share the man you love. It can easily turn a person into a murderer or schemer, dangerous, edgy and unhappy."

"I know, don't I know it," I said to my friend as she wiped away the warm tear flowing down my cheek, just as she had done when we were children.

"How would you know?" she asked. "Did you ever live among the kuma like I did? Do you know for instance that on one occasion my mother attacked Cevahir Ana? Cevahir appeared to like me but you can't imagine the dreadful things she used to do to my mother. It was as though the poor soul had to put up with two mothers-in-law at once. My grandmother found Makbule for my father when I was three because my mother hadn't given him a son. My dear mother suffered a lot it seems. I remember her often complaining about her mother-in-law daring to get Makbule as a kuma while she was still a young bride."

"Didn't your father object, Zelo?"

"My grandmother was quite a tyrant; once she put something in her head no one could oppose her. She was determined to have a grandson from each of her sons and that was all there was to it."

"Oh my God!"

"You can say that again! She was determined that her family lineage would not die out. You know, in those parts where we lived there are vendettas all the time. She was adamant that if a member of her family should die there would definitely be someone to take over. She was obsessed with the whole idea. Little did she know that being continuously at loggerheads with her daughters-in-law would lead to her downfall."

"But surely Kader Ana could have had another baby, why didn't she?"

"She did try but she kept on having miscarriages. My grandmother plainly enjoyed taunting her daughters in law even more than wanting grandsons. Apparently she had suffered a lot with her mother in law and wanted some perverse revenge. That's the way it is with us, Nevo. The poor daughters in law are forever being crushed and oppressed so that eventually when it is their turn to be mothers in law they take their revenge. If you ask me its revenge against their destiny. Sadly my mother was no different either when Makbule came into the family she co-operated with Cevahir Ana to make her life a misery. Before poor Makbule could even get pregnant, father was shot. Makbule stayed with us for a couple of years and then she returned to her father's house. I believe someone had asked for her hand in marriage but I can't remember the details. I just remember her pushing me on the swing hanging from the oak tree behind our house and singing sad folk songs. She was barely more than a child herself… I couldn't pronounce her name properly, apparently I called her Makana. Poor Makbule Ana, I wonder where she is now. I'm sure, I wouldn't recognise her even if I saw her. Anyway, all that was simply to say that being a kuma, sharing your husband with another wife, is really difficult to cope with."

Needless to say, it wasn't necessary for one to live under the same roof with a kuma to understand the pain she describes. It was enough to fall in love with a married man to identify with that pain. Knowing that the man you love and want to be with was cuddling up to another woman was like having your heart branded with a hot iron. It's enough to shatter your pride. It was difficult to share the man you loved whether you were his wife, lover or kuma. I wondered if Zelha would understand me if I told her that. In my case, I was the other woman, the kuma if you like and it was just as hard for me.

"How did you meet that married man?" she asked.

"We were working for the same company."

"The newspaper?"

"No, an advertising agency, I joined the newspaper later."

"Did you leave advertising because of him?"

"You could say that. I felt very lonely after my husband went to Holland, Zelo. Ferdi started paying more and more attention to me once he knew that I was alone."

"Ferdi you say?"

"Yes."

"Bloody Casanova!"

"Why do you say that? What has he done to you?"

"What was a married man doing running after you like that? He was obviously trying to take advantage of the situation… Anyway go on."

"I was scared that our colleagues might start gossiping and I felt that everybody was watching me closely. What's more I felt that if I started working somewhere else, his feelings for me might grow and he might start divorce proceedings…"

"I can't believe you were so naïve."

"How could I have thought otherwise, he kept on telling me his relationship with his wife was over?"

"They all say that. Were you in love with him?"

"To tell you the truth, I don't really know."

Zelha looked at me with amazement but I honestly didn't know the answer to that question. It seemed that her world was black and white, no shading at all. You either love or hate, it's good or bad, you can or you can't so therefore you are either in love or not. As for me, all I can say was, that, I thought, I was in love with him at first, or may be I was just filling that gap in my life. I might not have been able to leave him if I had been desperately in love with him but I might have confused her if I had said such things to her. After all, she has risked her life for the man she loved. She even considered ending her life when she found out that he had been unfaithful to her. Now she was devoted to her husband and loved him with all her heart. She might not be as passionate about her husband's quest as he is but here she was in prison because she believed that it was her duty as a wife to stand by her man and carry on fighting his cause. She was the sort of person who would do anything in the name of friendship, love and loyalty whether she thinks it's right or wrong…

"I'm still waiting for an answer."

"Oh! I'm sorry I got drifted away. What was it you asked?"

"I don't understand how you could possibly not know whether you loved him or not, Nevo,"

"Yes, I did love him but just how deep that love was I simply don't know. How shall I explain it to you? Well, for example, I didn't love him the way I love you."

"But I'm not your lover."

"I don't care, love is love. Just say I was to meet him some day after forty years, I won't feel as excited as I do now and if he and I were to speak, we won't have as much to say to each other as you and I have today. In fact, I'm sure that we won't even care about each other's lives. What existed between us is gone and forgotten. It's over and done with. The fire he kindled has gone out. There may be a few smouldering ashes, but basically, it's out. I don't even want to know what happened to him after we split up. On the other hand, look at us sitting here; I want to know every detail of your life. I want to share every minute of it. Do you know why, Zelha?"

"Why?"

"Because, my love for you hasn't diminished at all in spite of the missing thirty odd years. You're a true friend and I cherish that friendship."

"It's the same for me, too, Nevo. I want to know everything, carry on."

"I don't have that much more to tell, but, feel free to ask me anything you like."

"Did you leave him, because he wouldn't divorce his wife or did she find out and come knocking on your door?"

"Why are you so interested in those details, my darling?"

"In order to find out how much grief you had to bear and whether or not it caused you any embarrassment."

"But why?"

"Because, I believe that a certain amount of pain helps us to mature. The more we suffer, the more we learn to survive, somehow it makes us more conscientious... more sensitive."

"Well, you've asked for it so let me tell you and then you can decide how much I've matured. I'd be lying to you if I told you that I didn't know he was married from the beginning, I did. Like every married man, he told me that communications between him and his wife had completely broken down. He had even gone so far as to tell me that they no longer even shared a bedroom. I believed him, or maybe I wanted to believe him. Murat had been in Holland for months and my circle of friends had shrunk since his departure. None of the friends we used to spend weekends with bothered to contact me. Their sympathetic attitude and warmth towards me didn't last long. My loneliness was unbearable. So, it was just about then that Ferdi started coming on to me."

"How do you mean?"

My dear Zelo, I thought to myself. Of course, you're curious but, how can you possibly understand how a man courts a woman? As if tribal women are ever courted! I know only too well that they are simply ordered about. The command is short and to the point. So and so has asked for your hand in marriage, we consider him suitable, you will marry him and that's that. Done and dusted. Then when the man visits the girl's family bearing gifts and he looks into her eyes a little longer than necessary, that's considered flirting. God forbid you should fall in love with someone not considered suitable. Then the only solution is to put both your lives at risk because no matter how young you are, tribal laws dictate that, if you upset tradition, the penalty is death. On the other hand, our necking and flirting, not to mention couples living together before marriage, are all so very different to your way of life. How on earth can I explain all that to you? We are worlds apart on this subject that's why I decided to leave certain details out. I couldn't possibly tell her that Ferdi had been after me for quite a while before my husband went to Holland and, what's even worse, I had been enjoying his attention. Knowing how much she loved and respected my parents, I didn't want to tell her about their divorce either. The reason why I had skipped those details was not necessarily because it was easier to lie, but simply because, I wanted to spare her the disappointment.

"So you were curious to know how he courted me, weren't you? Well, it was like this. Every morning there would be a single rose waiting for me on my desk. Then he would send love poems to my computer. My colleagues and I would go out for a drink after work and he would join us. He noticed that I drank white wine, so every time he came he bought me a bottle of the best white wine in the house. On my birthday, he sent me a huge bouquet of long stemmed red roses; the delivery boy had difficulty getting them through the door. A little gift was attached to each rose… things like that… he'd say lovely things over the phone just before going to bed or first thing in the morning. He'd never miss an opportunity to give me a poem that he had written especially for me or buy me books he thought I'd like… one way or another he swept me off my feet."

"But he never divorced his wife, did he?"

"No, and I wasn't patient enough to wait for him to do it. I left him or I should say I sent him away to be exact."

"Good for you, married men never leave their wives. It would have been a waste of time to wait. How long did it last?"

"Long enough, Zelo. As I told you earlier, I even changed my job, so that I wouldn't always be accessible to him. That's when I got myself a job as a journalist. I had hoped that he would be jealous if I worked in a different environment with new people. I was wrong."

"Did you live together in your flat?"

"No, we never actually lived together. Cengiz was there at the beginning and when he left I didn't want to live with him because of my father. If he were to find out that his daughter was living with a lover, he would have had a heart attack, that's for sure! No, we lived in our own homes and sometimes we'd spend the weekend together. He very rarely spent a weekday night with me. For years, I waited for him to find the right time to tell his wife that he wanted a divorce. I didn't want to force the issue because it hurt my pride."

"My darling Nevo, I'm so sorry. It must have been heart-breaking for you."

"Don't feel sorry for me, there's more to come, wait and see what happened next. He had gone abroad on a business trip and he phoned me to tell me the date and time of his return. I left the office early that day. I rushed around shopping, cooking his favourite dishes and setting the table with candles and all. I got myself tarted up and looked forward to spending the whole night with him, because I had missed him so much during his absence. He arrived around eight o'clock bearing gifts of CDs, books and a bottle of perfume he had purchased at the airport. Then can you guess what happened?"

"No idea, carry on."

"He came in; glanced at the table I had so meticulously laid and told me that he wouldn't be able to stay for dinner, because he had to attend a most urgent meeting. Apparently, he had returned with a group of people who wanted to become partners in the firm. They would be staying in İstanbul for a whole week and that as well as having to have dinner with them that evening, he would also have to entertain them the whole time. He said that he only had time to have a quick whiskey with me; I was extremely disappointed but said nothing. I believed him. I had to believe him. I took the gifts from him and put them on the armchair. I gave him his whiskey and perched on his knee. I was eager to make the most of the short time I would have with him but there was something strange between us. I couldn't quite reach out to him. Every time I tried, he brushed me off. I tried turning the situation into a joke because I didn't want to get too heavy and I wanted Ferdi to enjoy his brief stay with me. Suddenly, I went quiet, I don't know exactly when or why but in the blink of an eye, the coin dropped. The bond between us was broken and I realised the pathetic situation I was in, everything became crystal clear to me, Zelo. I suddenly realised that he would be rushing off to the wife he professed not to have loved for years, had not slept with and didn't even want to touch. The woman he didn't want to upset by asking for a divorce. It became clear to me that he was going to go home to her, present her with gifts and apologise for being late due to an important business meeting. I realised that he was avoiding contact with me because he didn't want my perfume to linger on him, didn't want me to smudge lipstick on his collar and didn't want any stray hairs clinging to his jacket. I was simply an extra in a drama that he had written and directed himself.

Why I suddenly realised what had been happening for some time is still a mystery to me, it was as though a blindfold had been removed and I could see everything clearly. May be it was nothing extra, just the straw that broke the camel's back. Anyway, when it happened, I immediately jumped up and started screaming at the top of my voice, 'Get up and get out of here. Get out of my life!'

'I don't understand,' he said.

'I'm sure you do. Get out!'

'Have you gone mad?'

'Yes, I have. Get out before I empty this perfume over your head. Before I tear your jacket and rip your shirt. Get out immediately!' 'IMMEDIATELY!' I can't tell you how surprised he was; he was completely taken aback and didn't even bother to argue when he saw the look on my face. He got up and walked calmly to the door before I could shout again. I picked up the gifts he had given to me and threw them all at him. The book and CDs fell all over the place and the bottle of perfume shattered outside on the stairs. He rushed down the stairs shielding his head with his arms… I heard the gate to the block open and close before I closed the door of my flat and collapsed on the floor. I stayed like that for hours."

"Didn't he call you again?"

"Yes, the calls started the following day plus flowers, messages and telegrams. He kept calling late at night but I didn't pick up the receiver, I didn't even open the letters he sent. These kinds of gestures from him no longer had any effect on me; on the contrary, I found his behaviour over the top and immature. I even got a message via a mutual friend to say that he had moved to a new flat and had started divorce proceedings, so would soon be free to get together again with me. It was too late to start all over again, the magic there once was had vanished."

"Did he get that divorce?"

"I don't know and I really don't care."

Zelha stretched her arms over the table and stroked my cheeks affectionately. I was mumbling that I couldn't care less what happened to him; after all he was the reason why I had ended up alone without my husband, my son and most of my friends.

"Sorry, I couldn't quite make out what you were saying."

"I said I presume he went back to his wife, that's all."

I was too embarrassed to admit to my friend that it wasn't the food mixer that had caused my break up with my husband and it wasn't even Ferdi. It was my mother's fault. I had hardly ever wanted to be with her or even see her and it wasn't until the day she died that I realised how much she had influenced me.

After my mother left me and my father, I spent many sleepless nights gazing at the ceiling and wondering what she must have felt like when she went. Was she ever ashamed of what she had done and felt any remorse? Had her conscience bothered her at all and had feelings of guilt for the family she had left behind? Did she ever miss me or my father? I never told anyone about those endless nights tossing and turning with all these things racing through my mind. My father and I never spoke about her; it was as if we had made a pact to treat her as a taboo subject. We even avoided talking about her when Orhan came home for the school holidays. For two years, I had lived as though my mother never existed. I didn't phone or answer her letters. Then one day, shortly after I started university, she turned up at the gate. I was with friends and could only manage a surprised, 'Oh, mother!' She was calm and composed as if this had been a regular occurrence.

'I had an appointment around the corner and thought you might like to join me for a cup of tea or coffee somewhere nearby.' She had said and all I was able to do was to leave my friends and follow her to a local café.

'You could have let me know instead of popping up out of the blue,' I had said.

She pretended not to hear and reached out for my hand on the table. I had pulled it away.

'You are a young lady now; it's about time we got together. We should forgive and understand each other,' she had said.

'I've done nothing to be forgiven for.'

'You didn't but I did.'

'True.'

'Don't you think that if you tried to look at things from my point of view, you might find forgiveness in your heart?'

'No.'

'I suppose your father has filled your head with bad things about me.'

'My father hasn't said a word, mother, we never spoke about you at all.'

'That's even worse. I wish you would blame me and give me a chance to defend myself.'

'Of course, I'm blaming you; you were the one who left us, remember. You left us because you found someone richer than my father, didn't you? Go on, now defend yourself, what do you have to say to that?'

'It's my life, Nevra. Everyone should be able to lead their lives the way they want to. Your father did exactly that. He neither compromised nor made any concessions. He lives the way he wants to.'

My mother had put on a considerable amount of weight during the three years we had been separated. This dolled-up plump woman was right.

'You're right,' I said. 'My father never compromised his ideals and I am proud to be his daughter for that.'

'We're not all the same, Nevra. He had his ideals and I had my expectations.'

We remained silent for a short while with me nervously stirring the sugar in my tea.

'Can you understand me?' she finally asked.

I didn't reply. It didn't seem to matter to her whether I had forgiven her or not. Somehow I had drifted away from her. When she had first left, I missed her so much, I even missed her scent, but as time passed, the memory faded. It was as if a child had drawn a picture meticulously and then tried to alter it with an eraser but left traces of the original there. At that particular moment, however, the woman sitting opposite me was simply a plump middle-aged, over made up woman with not a hair of her bouffant hair style out of place. Her silly shit coloured designer labelled handbag was on the run down café table. I tried to feel something for her but felt nothing.

'Listen, my darling Nevra, mothers and daughters should not remain distant, we should be as close as a hand in a glove. You're older now, I'm sure there are things you need… I am your mother after all… I'd love to get you things that you need… anything…'

'There's nothing I need, mother.'

'Maybe not right away but one day… when you get married for instance.'

'I've no intention of getting married.'

'You mean there's no one in your life right now?'

'No,'

'There will be one day I'm sure. Wouldn't you like to be able to confide in me when that happens?'

'No.'

My mother stubbed out her lipstick covered cigarette saying, 'My stubborn little girl.' Then we remained silent again for a while before she suggested, 'Let's meet next Thursday for tea.'

'My classes finish late on Thursdays.'

'OK, maybe Wednesday or Friday?'

I said, 'Tuesday,' just to make it complicated for her. My brother had told me that she plays cards on Tuesdays.

'Fine, OK Tuesday it is.'

I was dumbstruck, I looked straight into her eyes saying, 'But I thought you played cards on Tuesdays.'

'If Tuesday is the only day you can make it I'll meet you then; my card game is not that important.'

She settled the bill and we got up to leave.

'You're staying at the hostel, aren't you?' she asked.

'Yes.'

'Would you like me to drop you off, I've got the car.'

'No thanks, I'd rather walk. It's not far anyway.'

She hugged me and kissed me on both cheeks while I stood motionless, like a statue in her arms.

'See you on Tuesday then,' she said in a sullen voice and left.

I watched my mother teetering away on her high heels. She always walked like that, small fast steps… like a bird.

We continued to meet up purely because of my mother's persistence. I was always reluctant; it was like going to meet someone I hardly knew. We would meet in different places but there was never anything particular to talk about, just idle chit-chat with someone you didn't really want in your circle of friends. I resolutely refused to go to her home or to meet her husband although I did meet him some years later at my wedding to Murat. He wasn't at all the short, fat bellied, small town Ağa I had imagined. He was quite a fatherly figure. I couldn't avoid visiting their home or inviting them to us because I didn't want to tell my husband about my feelings towards my mother and the barrier between us. After my son was born, her visits became more frequent but we never developed a real mother daughter relationship. She had managed to infiltrate my life for better or worse; there was no way that I could deprive her of seeing her grandson. I was no longer an orphan but I didn't consider myself as having a real mother, either.

My mother came back into my life when I fell in love with another man and like her, I became unfaithful to my husband. It was as if after a long passage of time, I had dug her out of the dark recesses of my mind and brought her back to me. When I was getting ready for work in the morning, making myself pretty for Ferdi, choosing my clothes, fixing my hair and make-up, it was then that I wondered if my mother behaved in the same way, slyly spraying perfume on her neck and behind her knees… did she also look furtively at her man from Söke the way I did at Ferdi? In the evening when I avoided eye-contact with my husband and especially the way I felt guilty in his arms at night, then I would think of her and wonder how she felt and behaved toward my father. Did she, like me, feel like jumping out of the bed? Did she feel suffocated? When I was giving the green light to another man while I was still married, I had hoped that I would be able to identify with her, but that didn't happen; those feelings just weren't there. I remained all alone in my shame and continued to feel distant from her. On the other hand, if I had been able to identify with her, I may have been able to be at peace with myself and forgive her. She, too had been bored with her husband; talking to her may have helped me to feel better with myself. I have never been able to understand how we reacted so differently in very similar circumstances.

Did I start my affair with Ferdi in order to better understand my mother? Did I follow the same prickly path as her in order to be able to feel the pain she must have felt? Did I want to get closer to that woman I thought I resented? I wanted to understand whether it was resentment or even maybe longing for the things I had missed. I hadn't been able to sit on her lap or sleep in her arms or smell the sweet perfume of her skin when I was growing up.

I would like to know if at the very beginning of my platonic relationship with Ferdi, I was, in fact, subconsciously comparing my feelings to those of my mother. Was there some sort of rivalry between us or was it that I wanted to take revenge? Why did I so desperately and relentlessly try to find out how she felt towards my father at the time? I had often tried to figure out exactly how old I was when she started to ignore my brother and me; when she sat silently in the corner without uttering a word to us. I vividly remember her screaming and shouting at us. That must have been when she had become fed up with being my father's wife. She was continually moaning her lot and feeling very sorry for herself. No way, I wasn't anything like her even though we had both committed the same crime. At least, I didn't nag my husband for a better life. She had one big advantage though, her man from Söke wasn't married, he was a widower unlike Ferdi. When my mother warned me about putting on weight, I switched from my usual gin and tonics to diet coke. I would sit in front of the television thinking of all the excuses Ferdi had used to chat me up. I would wallow in my happiness, although I knew right from the start that such a relationship had no future. I tried to keep a distance by pretending not to notice his attention and refusing lifts home after work. It was because he was married, I didn't really consider my marriage at all. Was it Murat's indifference that loosened the reins or was it because of my mother that I wasn't afraid of divorce?

"Oh, my dear Nevo, you big city women are all so gullible. You're ready to fall for any man that pays you the slightest attention with fancy words, flowers and gifts. As far as I'm concerned, the bloody bastard got into you're knickers and made you his mistress simply by buying you long stemmed roses," said Zelha who suddenly realised that I had drifted off. "Hey Nevo, I'm here where are you?" she shouted waving her hands in front of my eyes trying to bring me back to reality. My reverie in the past is broken and I am back in the prison cell.

"That's not fair, Nevo. A mistress is a kept woman, I'm not clever enough for that," I say laughing bitterly at myself. "No fancy cars, flats or furs ever came my way; we didn't even go away on holiday together. The most I ever got was a book, a CD or the occasional bunch of flowers."

"I suppose when everything is said and done, there's not much difference between women from cities, towns or villages. At the end of the day, we share a similar fate, we are the ones who really take the knocks. From what I understand, we've both wasted years of our lives, you waiting for this man and me running off with Alişan."

"True."

"What amazes me is that the men always get away with it; they never suffer the consequences. Have you ever heard of a woman living in the same house with two husbands? Or how about a woman who spends the weekdays with her husband and the weekends with her lover?"

"No, I haven't and I don't want to either. Believe me, I've reached the stage where I can't put up with a quarter of a man, let alone two. Thank you very much, I'd rather do without them."

"Don't talk like that, woman! You've obviously been hurt badly by this man and those wounds can be deep. You are aware of this aren't you?"

"Right now, all I'm aware of is that I am hungry, Zelo. Dilaver Bey said that he'd be around; do you think he'd get us some tea?"

Zelha gets up and opens the door and looking outside yells, "Is there anybody there?" I had bought five sorts of biscuits with me in case we got hungry, so I take them out of my bag and put them on the table.

"You can't trust these bloody men!" Zelha says. "There's no one around."

"Never mind, let's tuck in to these, I'm starving. We've been talking for hours."

"That doesn't surprise you surely; we haven't seen one another for years."

I teared open the packets and spreaded the biscuits on the table. Zelha immediately choose ten biscuits and pushed them in front of me. Then, she did the same for herself and looked me straight in the eye.

"Shall we?"

"Let's."

"Time me."

I looked at my watch, "Fine, you've got thirty seconds. Three, two, one, go!"

Both of us quickly started propping the biscuits up together trying to make little houses. Mine collapsed twice. She seemed better at it than me and managed to put a biscuit on top of the two standing underneath. I was the one who always won this game when we were kids.

"Well done, your hands are as steady as ever," I said.

"I used to play this game with my children, too," she replied.

I never taught Cengiz such games and even his bedtime stories were read by his father. My poor son was brought up by a mother who was full of herself, an introvert who was entirely immersed in her own world. I didn't teach my son any of the things I used to do as a child. I had so many regrets that I can't even begin to talk about.

"What other games did you play with your children? Do tell me Zelo."

"Do you remember that game we played with those little stones my grandfather had given us?"

How could I forget? And not only that... I remembered him telling us so many stories, too. He used to tell us stories he made up based on real events. We'd sit beside him all ears. He'd tell us sagas about the Kurdish chiefs who had revolted, illustrating them with folk songs from time to time. I used to love listening to him with my mouth wide open as he took me back to the days when the Kurds and Turks fought shoulder to shoulder to defeat the invading armies. I even used to dream about the villagers climbing the mountains pulling oxcarts loaded with rifles through the dark blue nights. When I grew up, I read about such things again in books. So many of the sagas were familiar to me.

"My God! What on earth are you doing, Zelha?"

"Don't you remember?" Zelha asked with a mischievous glint in her eye as she broke some biscuits into little pieces on the table. I knew that provocative look only too well.

"Of course I remember. Are you ready? Three, two, one, go!"

We both clasped our hands behind our backs, leaned forward and bowed our heads low on the table trying to scoop up pieces of biscuit with our tongues. The one who eats most pieces without using their hands would be the winner. We fell about laughing. If anyone should have come in now, they'd think we'd gone bonkers.

"Do you remember how Kader Ana gave us a beating for doing this?" I said.

"I'm more concerned about the wardress here; she's sure to punish me for this. You're OK, you'll be gone, but she's sure to blame me for this mess."

The table was covered with crumbs and the door suddenly opened while we are still grazing like sheep.

We were so embarrassed at having been caught, red-handed and quickly straighten up.

"I wanted to ask you ladies if there was anything you needed… For the love of God, what's this mess?" Dilaver Bey asked looking as surprised as we were.

"The biscuits were broken…" I replied.

"Well, clear it up as soon as you..."

"Would it be possible to have some tea?" Zelha interrupts.

"The canteen is closed on Sundays, but I'll see what I can do, Zelha Hanım, but in the meantime, make sure to clear this mess."

"Could you possibly get us some paper serviettes or something?"

Dilaver Bey looked reprimanding as he went out and closed the door behind him. We fell about laughing hysterically the way we always did as children. We used to laugh so much that we'd end up with stomach cramps. I took some paper tissues out of my bag.

"You're like a quartermaster, sergeant in charge of supplies, what else have you got in that bag?"

"A couple of apples, would you like one?"

"Not now thanks, maybe later."

Zelha held one of the tissues at the edge of the table and brushed the crumbs into it with the other hand and then swept the rest on to the floor with another tissue.

"You were always so meticulous and tidy"

"I had to be, didn't I? Otherwise my mothers would have given me a spanking."

"I used to be told off, too, but I could never be as organised as you."

"So what? I bet, you've got someone tidying up after you now anyway."

"Tell me the truth, Zelo. Do you really think I'm totally useless?"

"How can you say that, my darling?" Zelha said, walking round the table to me. She put her hands on either side of my head, pulled it on to her shoulder and rocked me from side to side. "You were the kindest child on earth; you had a heart of gold. I shall never forget the day I met you; I was wearing the galoshes my mother had forced me to wear over my shoes and what I thought was my smart, ankle length velvet dress. I'll bet I was the only Kurdish girl who had ever set foot outside the farm... and there you were, the daughter of the district governor with bows in your hair like a fairytale princess... I had expected you to push me around. In fact my mother had warned me not to fight back if you did. You can imagine how scared I was when I came to your house... and what did you do that day? You shared your dolls, toys and paints with me... you never patronised me and taught me everything you knew for the next five years. In fact, I'm certain that I would never be the person I am today had it not been for you. I learned so many things about life during those five years."

"I learned a lot from you, too."

"Your heart was so full of love. Not once during all those years did we hurt or disappoint one another even though we belonged to different worlds."

I started crying yet again. What was it this time? Was it that I now realised that I did teach her a thing or two? Was it that I am grateful to her for having opened doors to a world I never even knew existed? Or was it simply that I had missed the warmth of a person who really loved me? After all, my son hasn't been with me for some time now and my mother passed away a year ago. My father lived in a different city and my brother lives in a different country. My God! How thirsty I seemed to be for love! Shamelessly so, I didn't want to break loose from Zelha's arms.

"Zelha," I finally said, "tell me about your children. What are their names? What do they do? Do they look like you?"

"Sadık is the eldest… and then there are the twins, a girl and a boy."

"Sadık… so you've given your son your grandfather's name… What's he like, does he look like you?"

"He did when he was a child but now that he has grown up he looks more like his father, tall and handsome. He's studying at the Communications Faculty of the İzmir University."

"İzmir, really?"

"Yes, he's using my family name not his father's because, how can I put it? The way things are these days we thought it may be better for him. Thankfully the judge was most understanding and agreed to the change without much fuss. Once the situation calms down his uncle says we can always change it back. Sadık agreed with us… he is very intelligent and easy going."

"Look, I have a suggestion. Why don't we give him my father's address and phone number? You never know they might get together from time to time… My father could become his shoulder to lean on. He lives in Urla which is only half an hour away from İzmir. What do you think?"

"Your father might not want to get involved, Nevo, after all he is a prisoner's son… I really don't know."

"Don't be silly! You know my father, your name always crops up when we talk about the past, he'll never forget you."

Zelha's eyes sparkled, "Why don't you jot down the address and number on this pad."

"I'll do that right now," I said. "He'd love that. He misses his grandson so much. I'm sure that it would be good for him too."

"Really, Nevo, do you really think so?" Zelha's voice trembled and her eyes were misty but she had more control of herself than I did. Was amazed at how easily I cried these days. My mascara must have been smudged all over my face.

"I must look like a panda."

Dilaver Bey returned with two glasses of tea and Zelha raced back to her chair.

"What's up?" he asked anxiously.

"Something went into my eye, probably an eyelash; Zeliha Hanım was kindly trying to get it out…"

"No wonder your eyes look so red. You look as if you have been crying."

"I'll be alright."

"Ladies, I've put two sugars in each tea."

"Thank you," we replied in unison.

"How's it going?"

"Fine."

"No problems I hope?"

"None whatsoever."

He hung about for a while then left when he realised that we were not talking in his presence.

"I'll pop in later," he said as he left the room.

"So what are the twins' names?"

"Daryal and Helin."

"What lovely names. Is your daughter as beautiful as you?"

"Who says I'm beautiful?"

"Come on, you know you're a dark, raven haired beauty."

"You've got this thing about being dark. I remember that you were unhappy because you didn't have dark brown eyes when you were a little girl. Was your husband dark?"

"No, he was fair haired, Cengiz has taken after him."

"Have you got any photos with you?"

"Of course, I have."

I took my wallet from my bag and removed the photos and showed them to her.

"In this one, he is about three and look at him here in his primary school uniform."

In the passport photo, I was showing her he looked like a little old man in his dark blue jacket that didn't fit him very well and his bow tie; his serious face made him look precocious.

"This one is more recent, Zelo. My father took it when Cengiz was there last summer."

Zelha was scrutinizing the photo of Cengiz holding a fishing rod on a small boat.

"I must say he's much fairer than you, in fact he looks more like your mother although there is a touch of your father there, too."

"Do you mean to tell me that he doesn't look like me at all?"

"Well, he does in the old photos... when you were the same age... Don't they grow up quickly? You know I miss mine so much, my greatest regret in here is that I'm not able to see them..."

"Don't you see them at all?"

"They do visit but that's not enough is it?"

"No it isn't, and don't I know it. I miss my Cengiz ever so much."

We were sitting quietly sipping our tea. The feeling we share as mothers separated from their children was like a melancholic music only audible to the two of us. It was as though it penetrated inside us and plucked at the strings of our hearts.

"I wish you had photos of your kids with you. I'm so curious about them. I wonder if I should call them and explain that I am a very old friend of their mother… at least if I could speak to your daughter… Where are they now? Are they in İstanbul?"

Zelha took a deep breath before saying, "I wish you could, Nevo, but as I said before, Sadık is in İzmir and my daughter is at boarding school in Ankara. Daryal, well I'm afraid, you wouldn't be able to meet him at all, Nevo."

"Why?"

"He's too far away."

"Is he abroad?"

"Let's just say he's far away, Nevo. He's totally involved in this business, you certainly wouldn't see eye to eye with him."

"OK, then maybe I could contact your daughter, just speak to her on the phone and show some interest at least. But then… is she… how can I put it? Is she involved too?"

"No, not at all. All she thinks about is the latest fashion and enjoying herself. She's a typical modern teenager. I don't think she cares about anything other than having a good time. She's got her ears plugged into her music all day long jigging about leafing through the pages of those crazy fashion magazines and doesn't want to know anything about the cause. In fact, she looks upon those who are involved as lunatics. She can't understand why we bother about such things when we could just sit back and enjoy life. Frankly, I don't know how we produced such a daughter."

"Ah, the youth of today, Zelo."

"But the boys are young, too and they don't think like that. Especially Daryal... he's a militant... he's a tough one and no doubt, in fact I'm scared that he'll end up in deep water one day."

"I hope you don't mind my saying it but I think... what was her name?"

"Helin."

"Yes, Helin, I think she has the right attitude. After all, if she's not going to have fun at her age when will she? Would it be better if at eighteen she carried guns and grudges around with her?"

"There may be some truth in that, what happened to my youth? After you left, I suddenly became an adult, Nevo. I simply became one of the women on the farm. I did nothing but harvesting crops, climbing trees to pick the fruit, peeling potatoes in the kitchen and learning how to clean a house for when I married. In the evenings, I would sit embroidering my trousseau. Sometimes, I seriously wonder if Helin hasn't got it right. There'll come the day when she gets married and has children. No time for magazines and music then, that's for sure."

"Exactly, leave her alone, let her enjoy her youth."

"I do but unfortunately, Daryal doesn't leave her alone. As soon as the school term ends, he has her sent to the village where their grandmother lives. He even confiscates her mobile phone, can you believe that? He's quite a terror. The blessed boy behaves exactly as if he were a head tribesman."

"What right does he have to meddle with her life in this way? How old is he for God's sake?"

"He's her older brother after all."

"I thought you said they were twins."

"Yes, they are, but he's considered to be the eldest of the two. You know how boys behave where we live. Their word is their sisters' command."

"What about your husband. What does he have to say about all this?"

"My husband is in such a state, Nevo; the poor man has so many responsibilities, he doesn't know which way to turn. He has no time at all to deal with the children."

"How about Sadık? Is he like the grandfather you named him after?"

"Yes he is. He's a philosopher just like his grandfather. He's all for peace. All he wants is a proper job when he graduates from university. So, you see my children are all individuals. All I can hope for as a mother is that with God's will my daughter gets married so that…"

"So that you no longer feel responsible for her, I suppose."

"Whatever makes you say that?"

"Isn't that what all mothers want for their daughters, a good marriage so that someone else can take care of them? Then they can live with a clear conscience."

"I don't necessarily agree."

"Why not? Actually, do you want to known exactly when I realised this?"

"When?"

I was just about to say that my mother never was responsible for me when I remembered that I hadn't told Zelha about my parents' divorce. I swallowed my words and kept quiet. I wondered if I should tell Zelha the truth now that the opportunity had presented itself, but I decided against it. Zelha had created such a myth in her head about my family. As far as she was concerned, we were the perfect family; a righteous father, a beautiful mother and two sweet children! The family I missed for most of my life existed only in Zelha's mind. That being the case I decided that the ideal family that Zelha held in her mind should be allowed to live on. When I remained silent Zelha didn't push me for an answer, she drifted off, much as I had done, and I presume, was thinking about her children; the uncontrollable Helin, Daryal the rebel and Sadık the philosopher, three totally different children. I started thinking about my brother Orhan…

Orhan almost disappeared from my life when my parents divorced. My baby brother who I considered as my child because of our age gap had started to go to primary school when we were parted. I used to see him only during his summer holidays when he came for short visits. He was very introverted and didn't speak very much. I suppose he must have felt tense in a house where his mother was never talked about. He was very distant toward my father, although it was me who had forbidden any mention of her. When I finally started meeting my mother while I was at university, he was going to a boarding school. Later he went abroad; so we hardly ever met. There were even times when I completely forgot that I had a brother and thought of myself as an only child, completely alone. We finally got together when my mother died and he came over from America for the funeral.

My brother was really shaken up by my mother's illness and her subsequent death. She had told him as soon as the problem was diagnosed and he planned to come over for Easter holidays, but she deteriorated rapidly. Within two months, she melted like a candle; she got thinner and shorter and was very frail. Her energy and joie de vivre that I thought would never expire and the spark in her eyes faded away and vanished. My mother wasn't dead but she wasn't with us either. Her beloved son wasn't able to bid her farewell; instead she passed away in her treacherous daughter's arms. I telephoned Orhan.

"There's no way I can delay the funeral until Easter, you'll have to come within a few days," I said.

"I didn't expect it to happen this quickly. Even in the worst scenario, it usually takes a few months," he said with a break in his voice. He was right, she even surprised the doctors.

"I didn't mean to be reproachful Orhan… I'm sorry, I'm rather confused myself," I said.

Indeed, I was very confused. I was desolate. After she was diagnosed with cancer, I had meant to make up for the way I had treated her over the years. I had hoped to be able to be kind and affectionate toward her for the rest of her life but she didn't allow me to. She neither permitted her son to see her in such a dreadful state nor me, no matter how late it may have been, to play the part of a devoted daughter.

At the funeral, my brother and I stood side by side at the mosque gate as her only relatives. My father stood at a distance amongst the crowd; he hadn't wanted to stand with us. My mother's husband from Söke had died three years earlier. Orhan and I shook hands with each of the mourners and accepted their condolences. There were many attendees of all ages; she had had a wide circle of friends. We didn't recognise many of them at all. It appears that most of her friends from the bridge club and her neighbours were learning of her daughter for the first time now.

"Oh what a happy soul she was, so full of life!" "Such a smart lady, always so well turned out and still so beautiful." "Oh, what a great loss to us all, especially for you two." "Please accept our deepest sympathy… our condolences… May Allah ease your pain…"

After my mother was buried, my father went straight back to Urla by bus the very same evening. Orhan and I returned to my mother's flat. A cheek to cheek picture of us taken when we were young kids was standing on the bureau in her sitting room.

"Can I take this?" my brother asked.

"Take anything you wish, please don't ask."

"Thank you, this is all I want. I couldn't possibly manage anything else on the plane back to the States."

"Don't let that stop you we can always find a way, there's always cargo."

"Thank you, but all I want is a few photographs and that portrait of her on the wall. Wasn't she beautiful? I'd like to think of her always as she looked then. I remember so vividly how she sat by her piano; how irritable she got with me for messing about under her feet while she was posing for the artist. The dress she wore was a much darker green; it wasn't like that at all…"

He could easily have been speaking another language. He was describing a scene I didn't know existed. I had no idea that my mother had commissioned a portrait or that she had a dark green dress. It seems too that she got her husband to buy her a piano.

"Orhan… did mother play the piano?"

"Not really. For a short while after it arrived she seemed keen to learn. A piano teacher was coming and going for about six months. Wait a minute I even remember his name, Kavafyan? Yes, that was it, Kavafyan. All she learned to play was that nostalgic old tune she used to hum to us as kids."

I walked bemused around the furniture I had apparently inherited. There were no memories I could recollect there. Nothing meant anything to me.

"I wonder if I should be jealous or envy you Orhan?" I said. "This flat is part of your world, not mine… I feel like a total stranger here."

"Now you know how I felt in our father's house, it was the same for me there. All I can remember of that place is the white cover on my bed."

I blushed as I remembered how I used to shriek at him whenever he lay down on that bed. "You'd better take off your shoes before getting on there!"

We stayed at my mothers flat for a few days to accept condolences from visitors. I'd go to work in the morning and then take over from my brother in the afternoon while he went out for a walk to relieve the stress. We'd go out for a pizza at a local Italian restaurant and then I'd go home. After four days Orhan said, "I don't really want to spend the rest of my week greeting people I've never met before and saying the same things over and over again. Why don't we get away for a few days together? That is, of course, if you can take the time off work."

That would be a great opportunity for us to get to know one another better.

"I'm sure I can," I said. "After all if a father can take few days off for child birth, a daughter should be able to take time off for the death of a parent, don't you think?"

We took my car and drove to Capadoccia. Even though we were of the same flesh and blood, I didn't know what to say to him and we didn't speak at all during the journey. I wondered if this was a good idea, how the next few days would pan out.

As we reached Capadoccia, its extraordinary appearance took us under its spell. It was snowing very lightly and the area of rock formations called fairy chimneys look like somewhere in outer space. It was as though we were on another planet in another galaxy. In this new environment, it was not necessary to talk in order to communicate. It was as if God had come down to earth and taken up a seat in the back of the car making sure that we could communicate without actually speaking. It felt as though we were speaking, but silently. Suddenly we were getting along; we had bridged that gulf that had existed between us for years. We realised it was futile to continue blaming our parents for everything, that was all in the past and must be accepted as part of life's rich pattern. We had finally realised that it was totally ridiculous to feel so alone in the world. Even though we lived miles apart in different countries we were still there for each other. We were after all truly brother and sister.

We checked into a hotel in Avanos on the banks of the Kızılırmak River. While the area is considered to be one of the greatest sightseeing places of the world, what do you think we did? We sat in the bar with a bottle of wine and started talking about every detail of our lives as if to make up for all those years of silence. We talked about everything, our ambitions, our hopes and fears, our first and last loves, our work, our partners, our children, everything under the sun. The only thing we didn't discuss was the damage done to us before and after our parents' divorce. We had sorted all that out silently in the car on the way there!

On our return I felt as if I really had my brother back, my dear Orhan, my next of kin.

I glanced at my watch and saw that it was already nearly mid-day and I haven't even started my interview with Zeliha Bora, not a single note taken.

"Are you running out of time?" Zelha asked.

"No, there's plenty of time left."

"Good, but I'm sure there must be things you need to ask me for this interview. We have to leave time for that, don't we?"

"There's one more thing I wanted to ask you but... It stuck in my mind ever since you mentioned it..."

"Go on then, ask me."

"You had said that it was your grandfather who had decided to send Kader Ana to us."

"Yes, that's right; because your mother had had a miscarriage... the baby was stillborn."

"But why someone from your tribe? Your women never worked outside their own community."

"Well, because your father had helped with Cengiz, he felt he had a debt to settle."

"Over what? What had happened to Cengiz?"

"He had disappeared."

"What do you mean disappeared?"

"It's a long story and we haven't got time to go into that now."

"But Zelha, if I remember well, there was no such thing as a missing person then. How come you don't know why he disappeared?"

"Come on, Nevo, maybe no one knew about the organisation as such then, but I can assure you it had existed for years."

"Really!"

"Of course. There was censorship of the press then, so the man in the street knew nothing about Cengiz. My grandfather explained it all to me."

"When did he tell you all about this?"

"I told you that I had stayed with my grandfather when I returned to the farm after I had left Alişan. The evenings seemed so long and I couldn't get to sleep. Neither could my grandfather, the poor old man suffered with bouts of severe coughing. I used to roam about the house like a ghost and when he heard me, he'd get up and join me. He'd light the stove and put the teapot on it to brew some tea and then turn over the embers in the brazier. We'd make ourselves comfortable on the divan and spend the long hours of the night drinking tea with him smoking away. It was during one such night that he told me the whole story. He had a never ending supply of stories to pass those nights. One day, he'd tell me about the battle of Çaldıran and then continue with the Dersim events. On another evening, he would discuss his being exiled to Konya and talk about the disappearance of Cengiz. He talked so much about those heroic Kurds that I remember most of it off by heart."

We both started laughing.

"Come on then, tell me all about those heroic Kurds, what happened to them?"

"Have you got the patience to listen to all that?"

"Of course. I've got the patience and the curiosity."

"You remember how my grandfather was a details freak."

"Don't I just!"

When I stayed at the farm over the weekends, Zelha's grandfather used to gather his grandchildren and myself around him regaling us with his memories. Not only did he tell us the stories but he embellished them with appropriate folk songs. We girls preferred the stories involving love and the boys liked the blood-thirsty war epics. These incredible unknown details would explain why the Kurds and the Turks both stayed together and confronted each other. What a pity, we weren't old enough to understand the intricacies of the situation at the time. Now as Zelha started to relate those haunting stories from centuries ago, I was hoping I might find the missing link that would bind us together. I was all ears while shaking inside.

DEDE

All of us children used to call the head of the family, Zelha's grandfather, 'Dede'. I can see him as clearly now as I did then, his loose white robe and the grey knitted waistcoat he wore over it. I remember very well his white beard and his croaky rasping voice, the result of years of heavy smoking. I can see him sitting comfortably on the divan with one leg tucked back underneath him. He is taking a cigarette from his silver cigarette case engraved by Erzurum craftsmen and carefully putting it into his Eskişehir stone cigarette holder. He holds it over the embers in the brazier and with a few puffs and a deep breath lights it. He stares blankly into the distance as if watching a giant cinema screen showing scenes from his childhood, youth and middle age years. He loves recalling the hardship and pain he had to endure throughout his life. Who knows, maybe life before and after death too were there for him to see?

"Our tribe has been bound to the Ottomans right from the very beginning." Zelha began to retell the story exactly as Dede had done all those years ago.

"I want you to have no doubts about this at all my beloved Zelha. Our allegiance to the Turks goes way back to the Battle of Malazgirt (Manzıgirt) when the Selçuk Turkish forces and their allies the Kurds led by Alp Arslan fought side by side against the Byzantines in 1071. This battle resulted in the defeat of the Eastern Roman Empire. My own grandfather never stopped bragging about it and often pointed out, with regrets, that although there was a time we had become a province attached to the Selçuks, the descendants of the Ottomans along the shores of Lake Van, somehow we never managed to consolidate that and become an independent country. We were always left ground into the dust whether it be by the Mongols, the Safevis, the Akkoyunlus or the Ottomans, the result was always the same; they all made us curse the day we were born. For some reason our tribes never managed to get together and defeat our tormentors. We were always too busy arguing amongst ourselves to settle anything else, after all there were the Sunni, the Shiite and the Alawis living side by side. None of the Kurdish leaders were prepared to recognise anyone who seemed brighter than themselves lest they became leaders. We flocked like sheep from one side to the other. One day we'd be on the Persians' side and the next the Ottomans'. Yavuz Sultan Selim defeated the Persian Shah İsmail at the battle of Çaldıran in 1514; twenty-five districts governed by Kurdish leaders deemed it necessary for their security to remain attached to the Ottomans. They decided that since it was necessary to serve in order to survive, it would be better to serve the Ottomans who believed in the same prophet and followed the same religion. These leaders even sent the following letter to Yavuz Sultan Selim Khan.

"We have accepted from the bottom of our hearts the dominance of the Sultan of Islam. We are honoured by the name of the Sultan of Islam and began to quote the names of the four holy caliphs from the sermons. We made an effort to fight the holy war and committed to memory the teachings of the Sultan. We sent Mevlana, İdris-i Bitlisli, to you to plead for us; to help us your obedient and faithful subjects. We live closely with our neighbours the Kızılbaş but these pagans have burnt our houses and were at war with us. We are awaiting your compassion to save us from the cruel hands of these tyrants. We cannot fight them by ourselves without your blessing. Because, we, Kurds live in separate clans, we are only in unity in the name of Allah and are subjects of Mohammed. We can never agree amongst ourselves on any other matter."

It is important to consider carefully whether this letter was a good idea or not, my darling. When Yavuz Sultan Selim Khan received it from the Sunni Kurds, who considered themselves attached by the umbilical cord to the Ottomans, he reacted immediately. He took it upon himself to protect them from the Shiite and Alawi Kurds and also attacked the Kızılbaş in Eastern Anatolia. He slaughtered every last one of them, thus intimidating the Persian Shiites and causing the different clans of Kurds to become arch enemies. What can one say, at the end of the day, I suppose that we all have to pay for our mistakes but never forget, Zelha my darling, that most of the problems in the world today are based on religion. The older I get, the more I feel that people would get along far better without the interference of religion. I really do believe this. One more thing before I forget… as if it were not enough that our people were divided by different sects they were also divided by official borders, too. When Sultan Murat IV re-conquered Baghdad in 1638, the Kasr-ı Şirin Treaty was signed and Kurds were divided yet again. Those living on Ottoman soil were separated from those living on Persian soil... Can you imagine what upheaval that conquest caused my beloved Zelha? It literally put a formal border between our people."

While I was listening to Zelha, the endless folk songs Dede taught us to sing in unison, echoed through my mind. I mumbled them to myself, "Hot, hot, hot, hot..." That one accompanied the epic story of the Kurdish leader Sürmeli Mehmet Pasha; he won an important battle and then went on to slay a dragon… Very soon Zelha joined in with me and we continued singing about the natural beauty of the shores of Lake Van, waving our arms above our heads and swaying in our chairs. My knowledge of the Kurdish language slowly came back as we sang the lyrics. It surprised me just how much I did remember. When Zelha finishes singing, she continued with Dede's stories. My mind stayed in the Sarıcadam of my youth, I could clearly hear the drums and flutes played at weddings and I'm joining in with the villagers as they enjoyed their local dances. Then I was jumping over the fire with the other children during the early May Spring festival. In the evenings the older girls would scrabble in the earth to bury pieces of paper with the names of their loved ones scribbled on them in the hope that their wishes came true. Those girls who were afraid that their parents would find their secret often gave the papers to us younger ones to bury. I distinctly remember one such occasion when I was scratching in the dirt and suddenly I was lifted bodily by the strong hands of Cevahir Ana, somehow Zelha had managed to escape when she saw her mother approaching.

"Let's see what you're hiding under that bush you little madam you…!"

"It's nothing…"

Cevahir Ana ditched in the earth and found the piece of paper I had buried there.

"Is this your nothing?" She said holding out the paper.

"I only buried my wishes, Cevahir Ana."

"What sort of wishes have you got at your age?"

"Well… err… something."

She held out the paper to me and said, "Read it to me!"

How could I possibly tell her the name of the guy Hediye loved? I look up foolishly into the face of this powerful woman waiting for my answer.

"If you don't read it, I can always get someone else to read it for me," she said reaching for the paper again.

"I wished for a bicycle… yes, a bicycle," I mumbled.

"A what?"

"A bicycle, you know what that is, don't you Cevahir Ana? You know, that thing on wheels that the boys ride on. I'm sure you've seen them. Anyway that's what I wished for."

"Well I never... girls riding on those things, what next?"

"They do, but my father won't buy me one. I've begged him to, but he won't so I decided to wish for one, that's all. They told me that if I wrote my wish down and buried it under the rose bush, it would come true," I babbled out.

"Don't hold your breath young lady, that's an impossible wish. Off you go now and straight to bed with you."

I crumple, up the paper and put it in my pocket. Just wait till I catch up with that little swine Zelo. She could have warned me before she ran away. I ran straight home to find Hediye waiting for me by the door; she was flushed with anxiety.

"Did you tell Cevahir Ana what I had written?" she asked.

"No," I reply taking the muddy paper out of my pocket and giving it back to her.

She hugs and kisses me on the cheeks.

"Thank you sister."

"I'll go back and bury it later."

"No, please don't. Go to bed now."

I worried that poor Hediye's wish won't be granted because of me. I had tears in my eyes.

"It'll be alright, I'll go back when everybody's asleep."

Hediye stroked my hair, "Sibe, sibe… go to bed little one," she said.

By the time I started listening to what Zelha is saying again, she seemed to have arrived at the point in the story where the Emir, the Chief of Botan, Bedirhan Bey, had revolted.

"It's thanks to Bedirhan Bey," Zelha said imitating her grandfather's tone of voice, "that the Kurds managed to get their act together for the very first time. They united and made their voice heard and then what do you think they did, my darling? They gave hell to the Nestorians – the Christians in other words. Let me tell you why my beloved Zelha."

It was as though he was right there in front of me sitting on the divan with one leg crossed under him and stoking the embers in the brazier. For a split second the flames flared up and turned his wrinkled face a wonderful bronze colour. He took a deep breath, cleared his throat and continued. Once he started, there was no stopping him, that's for sure!

"Back in the 19th century Mahmut II in his Reform Decree promised to protect the lives and property of all his subjects, Muslims, Christians and Jews alike. There would be equitable taxation, legislative councils and a fair system for all. However, these worthy intentions paved the way for a rift between the Ottomans and the Kurds... Listen to this very carefully Zelo, I'm not saying between the Kurds and the Turks my pet... you see in those days there was no difference between a Turk and a Kurd, both were equally oppressed and ill-treated... in fact the Ottomans were considered the nightmare of all the peasants living in Anatolia at that time; the Turks, the Kurds, Armenians, Nestorians, Keldanis, Syriacs and the Greeks alike. Wait a minute, wasn't there a saying about this in the old days?... Let me see now... yes I remember, the peasants used to say, 'The Ottomans are never around when its time to sow or harvest but they're sure to be there when its time to eat.' Anyway, as I was saying, when as a result of the reforms the non Muslim minorities started abusing their rights, aided I must say by foreign intrigues, they started bleeding the Ottomans dry like leeches. Then, suddenly in the eyes of the palace in Istanbul the Turks and the Kurds gained esteem because they were the only Muslims."

Dede took a deep breath again and cleared his throat while at the same time puffing from his long cigarette holder. "Where was I dear girl?... Oh yes, the rights bestowed on the minorities by Mahmut's decree and the support they received from the British and the Americans. As a result of all this, these Christians strutted about as if they owned the country. The Ottomans didn't like the situation but their hands were tied, they couldn't even afford to pay their own clerks. They had accumulated debts upon debts by borrowing money from European banks. Pernicious advice from evil counsellors aided by the foreign intrigues paved the way for the Ottomans to drown in debt and become totally devastated. American missionaries started building huge stone buildings on Ottoman soil, on top of the hills where we lived. And what do you think they were building? Schools! I ask you, as if there were any American children living in Anatolia at that time. No, they were schools for our children where they could educate them in their ways and turn them into supporters. And that's not all, there's more... Listen to me very carefully dear Zelha... The next thing these so called missionaries did was to spread all over Anatolia giving support to the Nestorians and more or less putting them in charge of us. Thus these Nestorians now became so strong, that they were in a position where they might declare their independence and form their own nation. Can you believe that? Who the hell were they to dare such a thing and on this land, too! Didn't this land belong to us all? We've been living here together for centuries, Muslims and infidels alike but now with all this 'missionary' help these Nestorians decided that they shouldn't pay their taxes to Muslim Kurdish chiefs, causing thus, big trouble. How was a Kurdish chief to pay taxes to the Ottomans if he couldn't collect the tax from his people? The chief responsible at the time was Bedirhan Bey and this is what prompted him to unite the Kurds; and unite them he did as they were well and truly ready to teach these Nestorians a lesson. And what a lesson, they gathered together and marched on the Nestorians slaughtering thousands much the same as Sultan Selim had done to the Alawis killing the lot in one night. Some sources say that 6,000 Nestorians were killed, others say 10,000. The Ottomans were pleased to hear these reports, but what difference would it make when they were so deeply in debt? To make matters worse for them the Ottoman forces had been defeated by İbrahim Paşa in Egypt paving the way for the British and French to issue ultimatums to the Ottomans. Either Bedirhan Bey's forces should be silenced or the Ottomans would suffer awful repercussions. What could the Ottoman do against such an ultimatum? In a desperate attempt to save their skin, certainly not for the sake of the Nestorians, they crushed Bedirhan's forces. One may say that by doing this, the Ottomans had poured water over the fire that had been kindled by Bedirhan Bey, but he was not to be forgotten; he had gathered the Kurds together and sparks of that fire started other fires of hope here and there. It is true that nothing much came of that campaign but it did show that the Kurds could unite should the need arise."

I interrupt, Zelha's flow, "Come on Zelha, if Dede really believed that he must have been a bit naïve, mustn't he? I mean, I ask you now, is it the soil in Anatolia or the water that feeds this character in people? I don't know, but one thing for sure is that they are all pretty fractious, aren't they? He talks about the Kurds who couldn't even get it together under Bedirhan Bey. And what about the Turks? How different from the Kurdish tribes were the sixteen different Turkish nations? Tell me, is there anywhere in the world where so many different nations stem from one single tribe? I remember how we dreaded our history exams, because we had to memorise all those different principalities in Anatolia; Dulkadiroğulları, Ramazanoğulları, Germiyanoğulları, the sons of this, the Sons of that. Akkoyunlu's, Karakoyunlu's. My God! So many of them, I couldn't memorise them all and I remember thinking as a student, why the hell did you all keep on splitting up and fighting each other instead of uniting together? If they had done, I wouldn't have to remember all those names and dates! Surely you can see the parallel between Kurds and Turks. You Kurds are no different from us and what's more? Your tribes are still fighting each other."

Zelha tried to explain to me that the Turks were partly to blame for the Kurds not having their own nation. I listened to my kind-hearted naive friend without making any comments; she could be so easily influenced by the people she loved. This was one of the main differences between us. I wonder if my tolerance was due to the fact that I myself, have been one of those left-overs from a once mighty empire. Perhaps tolerance was in our genes. We, Turks, have never learned to blame others for our misfortunes. For instance, it has never occurred to me to blame others for the in-fighting between the various old Turkish principalities thus leading to their total annihilation. But, on the other hand, somehow I have already been the one to lament over the fate of the Kurds just like a mother who tries to cover up her child's faults. I don't know how or why I have been conditioned this way, but earlier listening to her relating her grandfather's stories, I did feel that we Turks were to blame for the Kurds' suffering. But then I asked myself if the Kurdish chiefs weren't also responsible for their people's suffering. I fully accept our share of the blame in what went wrong after Süleyman the Magnificent changed the taxation system. Previously, peasants had paid tax on what they earned from their land, after the change the local Kurdish chiefs set the tax at the level they saw fit. They borrowed money from money-lenders and passed on the interest charged to the peasants. Can we Turks be blamed for that, too?

I was not able to interrupt Zelha and pointed out that neither the Ottoman law, the Reform Decree nor the laws of the new Republic were able to stop the widespread corruption on all sides. Having only just met up again after thirty odd years, I didn't want to rock the boat any more by telling her that it was in fact the Kurdish Ağas, chieftains and tribe leaders who exploited their own people. I kept my mouth shut while she continues to retell her grandfather's stories with the same enthusiasm and excitement that he showed. I was dying to speak but was determined not to interrupt her, was because the sound of her voice was music to my ears after all these years. If only, we could spend much more time together.

During our cigarette breaks we hardly uttered a word; we were both too wrapped up in our thoughts.

After putting out her cigarette, Zelha turned to me again, "My dear Dede told me about the irregular Kurdish regiments called Hamidiye as well, Nevo. Listen to this…" she said attempting to continue with the stories.

"I know about them, too, Zelo."

"But did you know that they were set up to divide the Kurds?"

"Dearest Zelo, please listen to me. Did you know for instance that those regiments were set up to win back the Kurds, to make amends with them? In fact, at that time, the Kurdish chiefs were showered with endless gifts and medals and their sons were invited to İstanbul for special training. The Kurds were so delighted with all this that they called the sultan Abdulhamid 'Bavı Kurdistan' (Kurdistan's Father).

"And do you know about the atrocities perpetrated by these Hamidiyes when they were supposedly guarding the palace?"

"But they were Kurds?"

"Yes, but all their Generals were bribed, bought with money and titles. When the palace no longer trusted the Armenians, it set these brigands on them ousting them from their lands and taking that land over themselves."

In spite of all my good intentions, I finally feel as if I will explode if I don't put in my pennyworth.

"My dear Zelo, we're here together after so many years and I want to be sure that we are still good friends when I leave here. Please don't force me to argue with you by speaking like a child. You're saying that the Turks are to blame because, one, Abdulhamid built an army composed of Kurds. Two, he appointed Kurdish generals in charge of this army and three, the Turks are to blame yet again because they showered these generals with gifts, high ranks and medals. I hesitate to say this but you are forcing me to do so, you are insinuating that the Ottomans offered the Kurds the Armenian land, which is not true. It was the British who had the audacity to promise the land where Kurds and Armenians had lived side by side for centuries to the Kurds. This has been a dispute between yourselves and the Armenians for years and you're telling me the Turks are to blame for this, too! You had no qualms about occupying and enjoying those lands at the time and now you're lamenting the facts and blaming the Turks yet again... whenever war-crimes are on the agenda, these facts are carefully omitted. We don't behave like school children pointing the finger of blame behind your backs we treat you all exactly as one of us."

"Don't give me that, Nevo, don't pretend not to know that the Kurds attacking the Armenians was part of Abdulhamid's game plan."

"I'm not a historian but I'm sure that if one dug through the archives, one could get to the nitty-gritty, but let's assume you're right, that could be the case, then what? Have a heart; didn't the Kurds have any sense of justice of their own? Couldn't they have refused to carry out the massacres? Or, better still, let's leave history aside, let's consider today. Let's work out exactly what can be done for all the communities to live in peace."

"Even if we concentrate on the here and now, nothing will change, you will never accept the blame for anything, Nevo."

"Is it so important that one side is to take the blame for everything? Can't we agree that mistakes were made by all parties involved?"

"Hang on a minute. Just tell me who it was that forbade us to speak our own language, play our own music or even use our own names, eh?"

"Didn't we go through all that this morning? Didn't I agree that we were wrong on all those counts? What more can I say? Are you satisfied with that?"

"Yes I am."

"You see, we did try to rectify our mistakes even though we had left it a bit late."

"Only because of the pressure from the European Community."

"Possibly, but then look at the results. Anyway we talked at length about this earlier; let me ask you a question, too."

"Feel free."

"Why do you think it is that despite doing everything asked of us by the European Community they still reject us?"

"I presume they don't believe in your sincerity."

"Are you sure it's only that?"

"They're afraid of masses of uneducated Muslims."

"I see, they don't believe in the sincerity of masses of uneducated Muslims, masses who won't educate their daughters, women who give birth to nine or ten children, fathers who live by tribal laws that sanction killings etcetera. Chiefs who insist on living as if in the Middle Ages. People who won't work or pay taxes, people who won't pay for their electricity or water, guerrillas who don't believe in the equality of men and women and turn their backs on education... For God's sake Zelha, do me a favour, don't try to tell me that Abdulhamid is to blame for all this. Don't tell me that you have nothing to do with the European Community's decisions. Have we ever blamed you for it?"

"Are you telling me that you have nothing to do with the fact we have lived our lives as if in the Middle Ages?"

"No, I'm not saying that. No one can suggest that the Turkish nation is not partly to blame for the ignorance of the Kurds and their accumulating grudges. But then at least admit that you are indeed very stubborn in your ways. It's not easy to change you."

"Please note, Nevo, that this has developed into 'you and us' again."

"A few minutes ago, you said that the European Community did not trust 'your' sincerity, therefore you started it not I."

"My God! I can't believe that you've taken offence at that."

"Why not? You could have said 'our' sincerity."

"I meant the Turkish Republic when I said that."

"And aren't you a citizen of that republic?"

"Merely a second class citizen."

"How on earth can you say that when you became an MP in the Assembly?"

"Yes, but I didn't get very far, I was arrested at the door and thrown in here."

Unfortunately I couldn't make any comment on that and kept quiet on the subject. We Turks didn't seem to be able to strike a happy medium, we swing directly from one extreme to the other and no matter where we end up we are always wrong. I avoided looking into Zelha's eyes. She calmed down when she saw the meek guilty look on my face.

"Don't worry yourself about me. At least I haven't ended up on the missing persons list like my cousin," she said.

"Here we go again, this is the second time you mention it," I said quickly trying to change the subject and ease the tension. Plus I wanted to find out what my father had to do with this matter. "Come on, Zelo, please tell me what happened between my father and your cousin, I'm dying to know."

"Fine, but you have to remember that all the information I have is from my grandfather, so I can't swear to the accuracy of the story."

"That's OK, just tell me everything your grandfather told you, that's good enough for me. Out with it, I'm so curious to know what was behind my father's relationship with your tribe."

"Whatever for, why are you suddenly so curious?"

"We haven't stopped talking since this morning and this isn't the first time you've touched on this subject. I want answers to certain questions in my mind like, why my father was always posted to remote locations, why he was never promoted which was one of the reasons for the breakdown of his marriage and why he was held in such high esteem by your tribe?"

"Don't exaggerate."

"I'm not exaggerating, out with it, tell me your grandfather's story."

"OK, you've asked for it so here it goes just as I heard it, word for word."

"Would you mind if I recorded what you say?"

"Why should I, go ahead you never know there may be a novel in there somewhere."

"I'm not a novelist."

"You never know Nevo; I wasn't a politician but look at me now."

I rifled through my bag and found the tape-recorder, checked the batteries, pressed the record button and pushed it toward Zelha. This was going to be interesting, just like the old days when she would mimic the accents and the styles of the people she was talking about. Zelha fixed her eyes on a spot across the room focusing herself like an actress about to go on stage. She cleared her throat, slouched in her chair, clasped her hands tightly together and looked at me exactly as her grandfather had done all those years ago when he wanted us to pay attention.

"'I wasn't even twenty yet, when I first took my Cemal Fehmi in my arms, he must have been about one month old.' My grandfather said as he started relating the story, Hüseyin was still being breast-fed by his mother, but I am sure he must have been over a year old since he was toddling about hanging on to anything he could reach. Thank God, we had no complaints, we were very comfortable, we ploughed our fields, fed our animals and were generally contented with our lives. Then suddenly one day, our lives were devastated as if a bomb had dropped on the house. A new relocation law had been announced and we were to be moved to Konya. I ask you my girl, how many more times would we have to move? Wasn't it enough that we had to abandon our lands when the Russian army entered Van in 1915? Hadn't we already left behind our fertile vines, our misty mountains and the clear cool streams to settle here? We sang the old folk-songs to console ourselves and listened to tales of injustice before finally getting used to our lot and settling in our new homes.

Then when this new relocation law came in in 1936, my father, God rest his soul, put his foot down and refused to be moved again thus upsetting the rest of the family. Well, I suppose with a family of 120 people you can't expect that they would all agree all the time. Anyway, apparently all my uncles followed the leader Sheikh Said and walked all the way to Diyarbakır that is except my father and his younger brother who stayed behind. There's still a certain amount of animosity in the family because of this. Even our family name is different from the rest."

"But tell me, grandfather, how come our side of the family didn't follow Sheikh Said," I asked.

"Dear girl, don't bother about that now, it's far too long a story."

"But grandfather, I'm very curious about this Sheikh Said."

"Why's that?"

"Well, he is a very famous Kurdish leader, isn't he and I'd like to know more about him just as you told me about Bedirhan Bey."

"OK, if you insist. Listen to this... All the villages of the young province belonged to this Sheikh Said."

"Where was that province?"

"A little further to the north of us, my dear. It's called Bingöl now. He was born in Palu and his family were originally from a village called Septi near Diyarbakır."

"What did he do for a living? Was he a farmer like us?"

"No, he was a sheep trader both learned and wealthy. Every year he drove ten flocks of sheep to Aleppo, sold them and returned with a bag full of gold. Apparently, he was a very striking man. He dyed his long beard with henna and applied kohl to his eyes. He wore a green skullcap on his head and surrounded it with a white turban as proof that he was a Sheikh.

A tall robust man, like me, he walked with a swagger and looked very young for his age. The number of sheep in his flocks always increased because the stupid villagers gave him some of theirs in the hope that he would provide a passage to heaven for them. What a clever man, he would even arrange marriages that would benefit his family making sure that his brothers, sisters, sons, daughters, nephews and nieces married into powerful families thus increasing his power and fortune, too. He was certainly a great Nakşi leader and, believe you me, far more influential and famous than the Nakşibendi Sheikh himself."

"Yes, OK, but if he was so good and powerful, why didn't my great grandfather follow him?"

"Because, we, Kurds, were not uppermost in his mind, he wanted to bring back the Caliphate and the Islamic laws. Furthermore, he was co-operating with the British bastards. In short, he was determined to save his own skin not that of the Kurds. Money is the root of all evil. If one aspires to such grand heights in the name of God, one should steer clear of life's excesses. There's no point in preaching religion when all you want is the best for yourself. The two just don't go hand in hand. There were rumours at the time that this Said person had been sent by God Himself to restore Islam in this area. Well, would he co-operate with the British Christians if that were the case, I ask you?"

"Very unlikely."

"Exactly... and yet he kept on complaining that our religion had gone down the drain and that Muslim women had lost their modesty and the new Republic had produced an immoral society. When one makes such statements and goes on and on, there is always some ulterior motif behind it. I believe that Sheikh

Said, who was obviously very crafty, had his own hidden agendas. My father taught me that his preaching's were very dangerous. While he was prattling on about our religion failing, the muezzins were still calling our people to prayer and the mosques were always packed on Fridays. The women of our tribe certainly behaved very properly and stayed in their homes just as they had always done. As for immorality, in my opinion, that has been there in every society throughout history. Of course, I was only a whipper snapper in those days but all the members of our tribe certainly knew what was going on around them and they talked about everything. Anyway, my girl, in short, our immediate family saw no sense in following the Sheikh and going away. That revolt was in 1925 a year after the Nesturian rebellion just when the Mosul issue was being debated, you know all about that don't you?"

"Indeed I do grandpa, wasn't it ours but then given to the Arabs?"

"That's right and that's when the British stirred up the Kurds and the Nestorians to fight for their rights in the area. Believe you me, the British are dab hands at manipulating situations to their own advantage. That became known as the Independent Kurdish Revolt and Sheikh Said had a hand in stirring that up, too. The Nestorian revolt was quelled in ten days and had the Sheikh taken advantage of that situation and said that his rebellion was for the benefit of the Kurds and not to reinstate the Sultan etcetera, both my father and grandfather would have followed him. Did the Sultans do any good during their reigns? Why should we want them back? My grandfather liked the idea of the new Republic and wanted to see just how it would pan out having no links with the Ottoman Empire any more.

My father and grandfather made the right choices. The Sheikh's invaders took Palu and pillaged Elazığ before moving on to Malatya and Diyarbakır. Despite the siege, Diyarbakır was well defended by the Turkish army. When the Sheik's followers smelled defeat, the tribe leaders changed sides and joined the Turkish forces. The worst day of the rebellion for the Sheikh was when one of his sons was killed during the fighting near Varto. The Beys of East and West Dersim and even those in Muş who were ready to fight for the Kurdish cause did not join Said. He was sending out mixed messages, how could anyone be expected to believe that his aim was for the Kurds, if his followers tied their Korans to their banners and went into battle crying out, "In the name of Allah and Mohammed"? For a whole year, he had been lecturing on and on about the new atheist journalists denouncing our religion in their columns. He claimed that the new regime was poking fun at our Prophet Mohammed, encouraging everyone to turn against their religion and cursing our ancestors."

"They hanged him when he was caught didn't they Grandpa?"

"Yes, they did."

"Poor man."

"Hmm, maybe but let me tell you young lady that if he had succeeded with his rebellion, it wouldn't have been to your advantage, that's for sure!"

"Why's that, Grandpa?"

"Because for one thing, he was against the Civil Law. He was against daughters having equal inheritance rights with their brothers. He didn't want that change brought about."

"For God's sake, Grandpa, men don't honour our inheritance rights, anyway."

"Don't say that, dear girl. At least they give you something to keep you quiet. Maybe you don't get the land you deserve but you get money, gold and animals instead. How bad is that?"

"Anyway, tell me what happened next, Grandpa."

"Sheikh Said and his men were hanged and we thanked our lucky stars for not having followed him."

"Enough of Said, Grandpa, you were going to tell me about Cengiz, your grandson."

"You're right; you're right... now where were we before I went off at a tangent?"

"Konya, your grandfather didn't want to go to Konya."

"Ah yes, Konya. Well apparently we insisted that we were loyal to our country, that we hadn't followed Said's rebellion and had nothing to do with his politics, but you try telling that to the authorities. They wouldn't listen and were adamant that we should be banished along with the rest of the Kurds. We had no alternative but to leave. Can you imagine leaving behind twenty seven villages and taking a journey into the unknown. Many said that Konya was a fertile place and that we should be able to grow wheat. We prayed to God that, at least we could survive there. Some tribes were sent to Ordu, Giresun, Sinop and Kastamonu on the Black Sea while others were banished to Denizli near the Aegean Sea and Edirne in Thrace. Those sent to the Black Sea coast were worse off than us. They knew nothing about the sea and fishing let alone the constant rain. And do you know why the authorities did all this? Well, apparently the young communists in the military schools had started stirring things up and they wanted to scatter any possible rebellious people as far and as wide as they could. Anyway, there was no alternative and we had to come to terms with it. We packed up our belongings got the kids ready and one spring day crammed into a black train that was to take us to Central Anatolia. When we got to Konya, we were given a farmhouse, a few sheep and a bit of land. That's were your father and your eldest aunt were born, God rest their souls."

"So why didn't you stay in Konya, Grandpa?"

"When the banishment law was repealed in 1948, they said we could return to our own regions. Bulgarian refugees had settled in our villages but they were so unused to the extreme heat there, that many of them suffered badly and had abandoned our villages leaving behind our homes, land and vines. This news put us in a dilemma. We had made the best of our new homes, we had fruit in our gardens and grapes on our vines but some of us still missed our old place. For days and nights, we chewed over the pros and cons of returning to our familiar red soil, our neighbours who spoke the same language as us, our home. It was just the same as when we had to leave Van and we kept on longing to return. Eventually we, together with a group of families sold up our homes, land and animals in Konya and went back to our beloved Mesopotamia. We soon settled in our abandoned villages and were happy to be back; our wounds healed very quickly. Some of us even got involved in politics. I did encourage a number of nephews and cousins to go to the Assembly Parliament; some joined political parties, others became government officials, but I remained guarding my tribe; after all the villages and people therein, homes, gardens and vines all need someone to look after them, too. You may well ask why, when I was there looking after everything I could not prevent the death of your uncle and father. My power was just not enough to fight against the tribal laws. Not only couldn't I save my sons, but I also got my dear grandson into trouble. I will never forgive myself for what happened to Cengiz. In fact, it is the pain that I still feel in my heart that has aged me so much. Just look how bent-over and breathless I am."

"Please Grandpa, tell me about Cengiz. It's so cosy sitting here by the fire. Don't keep me in suspense; tell me." I said.

I didn't know why my grandfather felt so guilty, but I was certain that a man like him who loved his family so deeply couldn't possibly be responsible for whatever had happened to his grandson. I am sure that he must have taken the blame for something he didn't do. If only he would spit it out, then I may be able to console him.

He lit another cigarette, shifted himself wearily on to the other leg and cleared his throat before continuing.

"Cengiz was working for the family transport company in the city. Cemal Fehmi was responsible for collecting the crops with his horsecart and loading them on to the lorries that would transport them to the city. Cengiz was responsible for meeting those lorries at the warehouse, off-loading the crops and storing them. I hadn't put him in charge yet, but I was training him to take over one day. Cengiz wasn't an ordinary peasant like us you see, he was quite educated… He had finished the lycèe. He liked western clothes and dressed well, shirt, tie, waistcoat and all. I was happy to see him taking the job seriously and going to work every day and it was a consolation for my wounded soul."

"Your wounded soul?"

"Yes my girl, my first wound was the murder of my son for eloping with the girl he loved and the second, the assassination of your father due to a blood feud. Wounded was my soul but the pain was not as excruciating as it was during the first years. I became accustomed to the fact that just as he gives, God has the right to take away too; we have to be contented with our lot. Life does go on and I prayed the Almighty that, at least the rest of us should have long and healthy lives. I prayed and prayed but sadly God ignored those prayers, dear girl…"

My grandfather's voice began to tremble like his hands. I put the patchwork blanket sewn by the women of the village, around his shoulders to stop him shivering. He was so old and fragile that I didn't have the heart to make him continue.

"You're tired, Grandpa," I said, "Let's go to bed now, you can continue tomorrow."

"No my darling, not yet, just listen to this. I want you to know this unforgettable and tragic story concerning our family. It's as well for us all to know just what an unpredictable, back-stabbing world we live in. I also want you to know exactly why I will never forgive myself for having thrown my dear Cengiz into the fire with my own hands. You may also want to know why I shall always feel indebted to the father of your friend Nevo, our honourable *Kaymakam*."

CENGİZ

Cemal Fehmi read the letter one more time before he crumpled it up and angrily threw it into the waste-paper basket with the accuracy of a basket ball player. He stared into space for a while before picking up the telephone and dialling the number he wanted. He waited some time before Recep answered the phone.

"Hello," he said, "I was beginning to think there was no-one in the office, buddy. Were you in the warehouse?"

"We were offloading some goods, Hasan's wife has had her baby; there were some complications, so Cengiz offered to take her to the hospital. As there was no one else here, I had to deal with everything myself."

"Hasan's wife pregnant again?" Cemal Fehmi asked in disbelief.

"Yes, this is number eleven... he won't listen to anyone. Apparently, it was a breach birth and the poor woman almost died. Anyway, what can I do for you?"

"I received another one of those bloody letters this morning."

"Oh no!"

"This is the third one, what should we do about it?"

"I really don't know, my friend."

"Tell your father that we should have a meeting."

"Certainly, we can drive to your place whenever you like."

"I'd better speak to my lot first. I must also inform my brother. I'll call you again."

"As you like."

"Is everything alright at your end?"

"Yeah... fine... for now anyway..."

"Maybe someone's playing a silly joke on us."

"Could be. I hope it is just a joke."

"The goods arrived safely then?"

"Yes, I was just offloading them when you called. No problem at all."

"I'll send five more lorry loads next week."

"Good."

"Fine then, take care of yourself my friend. Give my regards to your Father."

"I will."

Cemal replaced the receiver, got up and started pacing around the room for a while before bending down to retrieve the crumpled letter from the basket. As he straightened up, he yelled in pain realising that his back was playing its usual trick. He held his back with one hand as he tried, cursing all the while, to straighten up. He sat very gingerly in the chair behind his desk and unruffled the letter. He read it again carefully as if for the first time before crumpling it up again and this time, throwing it furiously into his right-hand drawer. He shut the drawer and locked it before dialling his elder brother's number.

His brother answered immediately, "Hello."

"Hi" he said, "I'm afraid this is going to upset you a bit. I received another one of those bloody letters today… This one isn't stamped; they must have slipped it under the door… No, I have no idea, frankly, I don't think it's anything to do with the Bismiloğlu's, we've settled our accounts with them, we neither owe nor expect any money from them… I'm absolutely sure; in any case if there were, they would tell us to our face. This looks more personal although they do mention some organisation in this last letter… You're right, we should not meet them but we must find out who they are… No I haven't told Father yet, I didn't want to worry him unnecessarily, but I suppose he needs to know about it… I was thinking of calling a meeting at the farm tonight to discuss the matter we can talk to him then, maybe he'll have some idea about how we should deal with it… Fine… I'll come over after work this evening… See you there, bye."

When Cemal Fehmi finished his work that evening, he unlocked the drawer, removed the crumpled up letter and straightened it out on his desk before folding it in four and carefully placing it in his wallet. On his way out of the door, he shouted to the office boy, "I'm off now, don't forget to switch off the lights and lock up before you leave and don't dare come in late in the morning. I want you here by eight so that you can air the place and dust the furniture before I arrive and don't forget to note down carefully any telephone messages."

As soon as Cemal Fehmi left the office, the scrawny kid sat himself down in his boss's chair by the telephone, "Can't he change the fucking record? I know what I have to do, why does he have to repeat it all the time," he muttered.

All the male members of the family were gathered in the *selamlık* reception room at the farm. The table cloth was laid on the floor and the women of the house were coming and going with trays, plates, dishes and bowls of food. Sadık Ağa who had dressed in his brown suit for the occasion and not in his usual robes, was sitting on one of the divans around the room. When all of the expected brothers had arrived, Sadık Ağa got up, followed by the others, and sat cross legged on the floor around the cloth before saying a prayer, so that the meal could begin. Everybody started slurping away at their soup with yoghurt using the wooden spoons that had been piled up in the centre of the cloth. They, then ate the rice and carved the leg of lamb with their hands. Some young girls were bustling about helping with the service. After eating, they all asked for coffee. One of the girls placed three pots on the brazier to prepare coffee for Sadık Ağa and his two elder sons; the coffee for the rest of the group was brought in from the kitchen by another girl. When they had all been served their coffee, Sadık Ağa nodded his head and the girls discretely left the room closing the doors behind them. When the men were, alone Sadık Ağa addressed his eldest son, "It appears there's some trouble, tell me about it my boy."

Cemal Fehmi immediately got into the subject without prolonging the matter.

"About fifteen days ago, a young guy who appeared to need a shave came to see me in my office. He asked for some money for some organisation. I asked him about this 'organisation' but he was rather vague, something about the great liberation he said. I told him that I had not heard of such an organisation. Apparently, it's a new set-up. I treated the beggar in a civilised manner and pointed out calmly that he should not get involved with such things. I explained that to this day, we have never benefited from such organisations, on the contrary, we have always avoided getting involved thinking that it would do us more harm than good. He almost insulted me and used abusive language so much so that I had to show him the door. Before leaving, he told me to reconsider very carefully if I didn't want to regret things later."

"Why didn't you get on to me immediately, my son?"

"Because I guess I didn't attach much importance to it at the time. I thought it just another young rogue trying to con us."

"But that was only the beginning," said Hüseyin. "We got a letter a few days after that. The letter said that we should get the money ready within a week and wait for them to contact us."

"How much do they want?"

"Three million."

"My God!"

"Exactly, that's just how I reacted, too. How the hell do I give some little bugger belonging to some unknown organisation three million? Over my dead body! I'd understand if he said he was desperate, a son needed an operation or debt collectors were after his blood."

"Maybe he was too proud to beg for himself and invented this organisation to get money," said one of the nephews.

"Could he be trying to blackmail us?" asked Sadık Ağa.

"That did cross my mind, too, but what is there for anyone to blackmail us for? We don't owe any money and all our accounts are in order I just rechecked."

"But, you have to be careful. If this rogue continues pestering us he could cause trouble."

"I have no intention of giving him any money but it looks as if he won't give up. Today's letter was the third and this one wasn't even posted, it was shoved under the door. What's more, he's increasing the pressure, now he's threatening that they will burn our lorries if we don't pay up."

"Who are 'they'?"

"The members of this organisation."

"Did you find out anything about them?"

"They call themselves The Great Liberation Day Organisation, that's all I know."

"Who the hell are the bastards liberating and from whom?"

"That I don't know, but I must admit that I got rather scared when they threatened to burn one of our lorries… I thought I should ask for your opinion."

"Please be very careful, Cemal Fehmi, don't get involved. We have lost enough members of our family to the Kurdish cause and tribal feuds over the years. I don't want to lose any more of you. Do you understand? And be careful not to rub him up the wrong way, don't even throw him out. Try and solve this peacefully. Talk to him tactfully. Tell him that our business is not doing so well these days. Point out that we are just about to pay our taxes. Fend him off; tell him we'll sort something out when things improve."

"Leave it to me," said Cemal Fehmi.

No one objected to Sadık Ağa's decision. None of the men were for handing over the money. They believed that if they all felt the same way, they would be able to sort it out. The meeting finished at about 10 o'clock and Cemal Fehmi went to his home in town.

Cemal Fehmi was feeling more relaxed the following morning when he went to work. Bilal had obviously been there for some time when he arrived because the place was aired and he was busying around with the duster. When he heard his boss come in, he stood straight up respectfully. His face was as white as a sheet.

"Why don't you close the window my lad, you obviously feel cold you're so pale."

"Sir, I am sorry to be the bearer of bad news but…" he mumbled, "I received a phone call a little while ago… apparently they called you at home but you had already left…" Bilal was trembling uncontrollably.

"What the fuck are you going on about? Can't you speak more clearly? What's happened?"

Before Bilal could answer the telephone rang. Cemal Fehmi seemed confused as he looked at the phone then Bilal and then back to the phone before eventually picking it up.

"Whaaat! What are you talking about?... When?... Why?... Totally burnt?... Who?... Fucking rogues! Bloody bastards! OK, I'm on my way."

He collapsed into the chair by the desk and dropped the receiver on to the floor. Bilal rushed over to pick up the receiver and put it back in its place. Cemal Fehmi sat motionless with his head in his hands for a while, then he spoke very slowly as if in a trance: "They burnt one of our lorries," he sounded exhausted.

"I know, Sir, they called before you arrived, that's what I was going to tell you."

"I'm going to the city. Close the windows lock up and go to the farm, but don't tell my father anything about this before I call."

Sadık Ağa's sons, grandsons, male cousins and nephews gathered at his business partner, Recep's house in the city. They were all shocked arguing and blaming each other for a while. Some said that they should have paid the money others were adamant that they made the right decision. When they all calmed down, they talked about what they should do next. The burnt lorry together with the goods it was carrying cost them more than the money they had been asked for. Thank God, that both the lorry and the goods were insured. What was done was done. They were all devastated but surely, they thought, the bloody thieves wouldn't dare to torch another lorry, would they? Finally, they decided to ignore the incident without even telling the police.

A week after the lorry incident another threat was made. Just as Cemal Fehmi was leaving his office someone phoned and asked him if he had learnt his lesson.

"We had come to the conclusion that it was an accident but now, you're telling me that you were the perpetrators. Fine, we have your confession but let me tell you that I am certainly not giving you the money now even though I might have changed my mind. The only kind gesture you'll get from me is that I won't report the matter to the authorities. Why don't you just admit that you picked on the wrong people and leave us alone. I'm leaving you to God's justice; I don't want to hear another word out of you ever again!"

Even though he spoke very calmly and convincingly, his hands were shaking when he replaced the receiver. He asked Bilal to make him a strong coffee which he drank while he thought things over very carefully. When Bilal had collected the empty cup and left the room he called his older brother. They had been speaking for a long time when their conversation was interrupted by Bilal who entered the room, looking very anxious. Apparently, there was a policeman at the door who wanted to escort his boss to the police station. Cemal Fehmi put the receiver down and leaped to his feet. He went to the police station where he was asked to make a statement about the incident. He did so without mentioning that he was being threatened. He claimed that he thought the lorry may have burnt due to an electrical fault in the ignition and that they didn't suspect foul play.

When he returned to his office, he collapsed into his chair and started telephoning the family with the latest development. They all agreed to adopt the same attitude and say nothing else. Furthermore, they all agreed that in future all the lorries and carts should have a security guard on board and that under no circumstances were the goods to be left unguarded.

The following day the political police got involved in the incident putting everyone on tenterhooks for a few days. Finally, the incident was closed when they concluded that it was indeed an accident caused by an electrical fault.

Another lorry was burnt 17 days after the first one.

On the same day, yet, another lorry carrying wheat to the Eastern counties rolled down an embankment, due to a brake failure, killing the driver.

When the family gathered again at Sadık Ağa's farm, this meeting was too serious to be conducted over dinner. This situation needed some careful thinking; their family transport business, their main source of income, had taken a serious blow. They all gathered in Sadık Ağa's sitting room with solemn faces. The relatives who joined from both the cities and the boroughs expressed their opinions one by one. Sadık Ağa listened patiently to all of them. His eyes were fixed on the floor as he considered everything for a while and then he addressed them all speaking with a solemn voice that reflected his anxiety.

"We have to give them this money, we have no alternative," he said. "If we don't, it seems to me that, apart from lorries we will also be losing lives. If we don't, I'm sure I'll end up being blamed for the death of the drivers. I won't allow anyone to say innocent men are dying because the Ağa doesn't want to part with his money."

"The bloody bastards are calling me every Tuesday without fail. I suppose, I'll have to give them a positive answer next time. What a pity!" said Cemal Fehmi.

"You can say that again but it seems to me that we have no alternative."

"I bet they'll want the money by the weekend."

"Can you get it together by then?" asked Sadık Ağa.

"Yes, we can," replied Hüseyin.

"Listen carefully," said Sadık Ağa, "no one outside this room must know that we've paid money to the bandits. And another thing, when you hand over the money, you'd better make sure they know that this is a once and for all payment. We will pay them, shake hands on it and this matter will be closed forever."

"Fine, understood, father."

"Do you know who'll come to collect the money?"

"Presumably, the same rascal that came to the office."

"Are you sure he'll hand over the money to the organisation and not keep the money for himself?"

"Come on, he can't do that, surely."

"Why not? He can tell them we didn't give him the money, can't he?"

"I suppose we could ask him for a receipt."

"Yes, that's a good idea. He can write that he received such an amount of money on a piece of paper and sign it. His own hand-writing and signature should be enough proof for us should the need arise."

"You're right, father," said Cemal Fehmi.

"One more thing, who's going to hand over this money to them?"

"I'll do it."

"No, you shouldn't. If the authorities were to find out, we'd be found guilty of supporting such an organisation."

"How can anyone find out if we all keep our mouths shut?"

"They say even walls have ears, so we should be extremely cautious."

"So, what do you suggest?"

"There must be a way around this I'm sure."

They all sat around for a while deep in concentration without uttering a word. Eventually Sadık Ağa told his son to ask the girls to make some coffee. "We ought to come up with an answer while drinking our coffee," he explained.

Hüseyin left the room and asked the women to make coffee. After a short while girls wearing velvet dresses embroidered with silver thread came in bearing trays and pots for the coffee. They prepared the coffee on the brazier and served the men in small silver cups. The room was filled with the scent of cardamom.

Sadık Ağa slurped his coffee noisily through his teeth but didn't drink much before putting it down. There was a look on his face which suggested that he wasn't altogether happy with what he was about to say. "Let's have Cengiz deliver the money," he said in a hoarse voice.

"I beg your pardon, father."

Sadık Ağa cleared his throat and tried again, "I said Cengiz, let Cengiz hand over the money."

"Why Cengiz?"

"For a start he's still young, he has neither a wife nor children, from time to time he misbehaves, he gambles and gets into debt…"

"But father…"

"Don't interrupt Hüseyin. I know that Cengiz is your son but don't forget that he's also my grandson. You may have tried to keep certain things from me but I am fully aware of what's going on. I have ears and eyes everywhere. I may be old but I haven't gone senile yet."

"How can you say that, Father?"

"Now then, where was I? Yes, I said that Cengiz gambles…"

"Not any more, Father. I swear he doesn't, he gave me his word..."

"Didn't I ask you not to interrupt me Hüseyin?... every cloud has a silver lining... in fact in this case his gambling may be an advantage... Let Cengiz deliver the money and if one day, any of this should come out, we can always say that the bastard was settling his gambling debts. We helped him to pay them off."

After the family had dispersed to their various homes, Sadık Ağa called one of his grand-daughters.

"Now then, my little darling," he said, "prepare me a good strong coffee the way only you can do it, so that I can enjoy it in peace before going to my bed."

"Of course, Grandpa," she said rushing to the kitchen.

"Wait, Hediye, wait! Come to think of it, I'd rather have a rakı'. Bring a carafe of water with it so that I can add the water to it myself."

"But, Grandpa isn't it a bit late?"

"It is indeed my little one, but I'm feeling rather sad at the moment, a strong drink will do me good. Some people calm down when they've had a drink, others go wild. I'm one of the former. I believe that I won't be able to sleep at all if I don't have a good strong drink."

"What's wrong Grandpa has someone upset you? Is there anything I can do to help?"

"No, my darling, no. I don't think you or anybody else can help me now. The arrow has left the bow as they say, who knows where it may land?"

"I don't understand what you are saying, Grandpa."

"Don't you worry your pretty little head, darling. Old people talk too much. Off you go and get me my drink. That's the best thing you could do for me right now, but make sure your mothers and especially your grandmother knows nothing of this."

Sadık Ağa waited for a while after Hediye left the room then, when he was sure she was well away, he went and stood in front of the window. He looked towards the rising moon and started hitting his chest with his fists and roaring like a wounded lion. "Blessed crescent of God, look at this state I'm in and take pity on me. Look at the way these scoundrels have brought me to my knees! Mighty God, what have I done to deserve this?"

***

In the lavatory of a smoky billiard room in the city, Cengiz made the young man wearing a duffle-coat write a rough note on a piece of paper to the effect that he had received a certain amount of money. Cengiz, who was sitting on the money, then handed over the package. The young man counted the money before adding his signature to the note.

"Now," said the guy turning to Cengiz, "I want you to write a similar note stating exactly how much money you've handed over and then sign it!"

"There's no need for that," said Cengiz.

"Oh, yes there is," replied the guy, "I want you to say exactly how much you've given me so that they can't accuse me of keeping some of it for myself."

"How will they know that it was me who wrote the note?"

"Don't argue, just write the note!"

"What if I don't?"

"Another one of your lorries might have an accident tomorrow, that's what, mister." He then took a piece of paper from his pocket, unfolded it and put it beside the sink before handing Cengiz his pen.

"What if someone should come in?"

"They won't, I've got friends guarding the door. Now, get on with it before I lose my temper, I don't want to spend the bloody night in this crapper!"

"Arsehole," Cengiz mumbled between his teeth. He wrote the amount on the paper and signed it.

"OK, now get your arse out of here!"

Cengiz controlled himself. What he really wanted to do was to punch the guy on the nose, but he just walked out slamming the door behind him. He walked through the cloud of smoke in the billiard room and hurried outside. He hailed a taxi and went straight home and phoned his father.

"All is done, father," he said, "everything went according to plan... I'll leave you to tell the others."

***

Spring was awakening in Anatolia. The hillsides were painted yellow with the flowers of the broom bushes, the daisies, poppies and forget-me-nots bloomed in the meadows. Nature adorned herself with the seven colours of the rainbow. Trees started to blossom and the sheep gave birth to their baby lambs. A happy commotion was taking place at the Kasrıkoğlu farm. Sadık Ağa's grand-daughter was about to get married. The wedding was to take place in the front garden. Some of the guests had been invited to stay overnight at the farm, so the girls were meticulously cleaning the floor in the back yard, so that feather mattresses and quilts could be laid out. All the other women were busy preparing the pastries.

Sadık Ağa had developed an allergy to the sound of a telephone ringing. He was busy dealing with his accounts when it disturbed him this time. Reluctantly he, picked up the receiver.

"Hello."

"Oh father... dear father... I've got terrible news. They arrested Cengiz this morning and took him away with them," Hüseyin's voice was trembling.

"Who took him away and where to?"

"Soldiers. I don't know where they took him."

"Why?"

"Because he paid the money to that organisation."

"I thought that was our secret. No one was to talk about it. I wonder which idiot squealed. Which God forsaken bastard... which..?"

"Hold your horses, father, it wasn't any one of us, you can be sure of that. Apparently, it was the rogue who collected the money who squealed."

"How do you know that?"

"The police told me."

"Didn't you tell them he was settling his gambling debts?"

"We did but it seems that Cengiz had been under surveillance at the time, father…"

"Why the hell didn't you let me know at once? Why am I always the last to know anything?"

"We didn't want to upset you; we thought we could deal with it on our own. He was released after the police had interrogated him the first time and sent home. A van full of soldiers was sent both to his home and his office. They ransacked both places looking for something or other. They couldn't find anything, but what was to find anyway. It was then that they took Cengiz away with them. His neighbours told me, that's how I know all this."

"Hüseyin, the time has come for you to tell the whole story to both the police and the soldiers. Tell them everything exactly as it happened. The burnt lorries, that disastrous accident, the threatening letters... everything!"

"Won't they want to know why we didn't report all this at the time?"

"Of course, they will and you'll just have to explain it all to them. You must save the lad."

When he put the receiver down Sadık Ağa clasped his chest and collapsed into his chair with his head on the table. "It's all my fault, Cengiz," he said in a barely audible voice, "I did this to you, I'm responsible..."

***

Cengiz woke up on the wooden floor of his prison cell. At first, he thought he'd had a nightmare, so, he closed his eyes tightly again before opening them to realise that this was no nightmare. There was just a chair in the cell. He tried to stand up but realised that he was aching all over. He struggled up and managed to sit on the chair. He remembered being taken by jeep to the city where the Command Headquarters was and then being handed over to a soldier who locked him in the cell. Looking at his watch he saw that it was three minutes past seven. He looked around for any toilet facilities but there were none. He tried to open the door to the corridor but it was locked so he banged and banged on it until someone came.

"What the hell is all this racket about?" asked the soldier who looked in through the door.

"I need to use the lavatory."

"Follow me!"

He followed the soldier along a long corridor and then down some stairs to the floor below.

"You'd better be quick about it," said the soldier pointing to a door on the left.

When he had finished he followed the soldier back to his cell.

"Have you any idea how long I am to stay here, brother?"

"I'm no brother of yours. I'm no traitor."

"Neither am I."

"So, why are you here then?"

"There must be some mistake."

"You don't say."

"I swear, I swear on everything that's sacred to me."

"Watch it!"

"Brother... sorry, boss, how much longer...?"

"I don't know, you son of a bitch. Just sit right where you are and thank your lucky stars." With that the soldier locked the door and left.

Cengiz sat on the floor and rested his head on his arms on the chair hoping to get some sleep as he was feeling very tired. He did eventually drop off only to be woken up by a booted foot kicking him. He hadn't heard the door being opened so he looked up and saw a soldier standing there with a bowl of soup and some bread. Cengiz sprung to his feet.

"Thank you, brother," he said regretting it immediately lest it be the same soldier, "can you please tell me how long I am to be kept here?"

Thank God this was a different soldier who didn't scold him.

"Until the interrogation is over."

"When will that be, do you think?"

"I wouldn't know. Knock on the door when you've finished."

Cengiz put the bowl of soup on the chair and sat on the floor before taking a bite of the bread. It was so stale, it felt as if he were biting stone. He didn't care because he was so hungry but he couldn't swallow it, so he broke off pieces of the bread and dropped them into the soup to soften it. When he tried to eat the softened bread, the soup tasted like dishwater, but he realised he needed something inside him to set him up for the interrogation and to stop his stomach rumbling. He now had some hope in his heart. He was sure that they would realise that he was innocent and they were bound to release him. No one at the police station had believed him when he said that he was paying gambling debts. This meant that it was about time to tell the truth. He remembered getting a glimpse of his father in the crowd as he got out of the jeep outside the Command Headquarters. He thought his father was signalling that he should talk. When he was locked up in the cell he wasn't sure whether it was his father at all or was he just imagining it. Or was it a dream? No, he hadn't fallen asleep by that time so it couldn't have been a dream. Did I see him, didn't I see him, did he say talk, didn't he say talk, total confusion rushed through his brain. "God help me keep my sanity," he prayed to himself. He must be ready for this interrogation, he must be sure of what he has to say.

Cengiz put the bowl of soup with the soggy bread in it on the floor and went to knock on the door. No one answered. He sat on the chair and started to think about why all this had happened to him. How come a young man with no political affiliations or views, in fact a young man who hated politics, became embroiled in all this. His only weakness was the occasional game of poker and what had that got to do with it? He put his hands in his pockets and discovered a packet of cigarettes. What joy, he had forgotten all about them during the commotion of his arrest. He pulled out the packet and opened it, his lighter fell out of it. What a good habit it was to keep the lighter in the packet. He lit up a cigarette and drew in a deep breath.

"This will pass, too," he said to himself, obviously feeling more relaxed after a couple of puffs, "it'll turn out right, in the end."

After two days of trying to eat stale bread soaked in cold soup, both his good mood and his cigarettes began to run out. On the third day he was taken to be interrogated.

"OK, Kasrıkoğlu," said a man in uniform, "let's have it."

"Have what, sir?"

"The whole damn story. Your relationship with the organisation."

"I have nothing to do with any organisation."

"Is that why you gave money to them?"

"I repeat I have nothing to do with any organisation."

"Look here young man, let me give you a bit of advice. For your own good, tell me the truth. If you tell me everything, not only will you be making our job easier for us, but you'll be able to walk straight out of here… But… if you take us for fools…"

"Please don't say that General."

"I'm not a General"

"Sorry, Commander."

"Listen to me carefully, my son. You're the one under interrogation here. We can interrogate you, but nobody can interrogate us… Do you understand what I am saying?”

“Yes, sir.”

“Are you sure?”

“Yes, I’m sure, sir.”

“Good, in that case just answer my questions and don’t be tempted to lie or deviate. If you lie to me or withhold information, we are in a position to get to the truth whatever it takes.”

“I don’t lie, sir.”

“In that case why are you telling me that you have nothing to do with the organisation?”

“Because I don’t, sir. If only you’d let me explain…”

“Do you or don’t you have anything to do with the organisation?”

“I don’t.”

“So you’ve made up your mind not to co-operate, is that it?”

“No, sir, I have nothing to do with them.”

“Have it your own way Kasrıkoğlu. You are entirely responsible for what’s to happen to you from now on. You can be crippled for life or even die after being tortured. Why can’t you just be sensible and tell me everything without me having to resort to torture. Believe me, I don’t enjoy it.”

“Yes, sir… well… you know we own some lorries…”

“I know that!”

“We use them to deliver wheat to the factories in the city…”

“Don’t bother telling me what I already know, tell me what I don’t know.”

“I’m trying to explain why I had to give them some money.”

"Aha, so you do admit that you gave them some money."

Cengiz shifted uncomfortably in the chair. He noticed the commander interrogating him kept on waving a piece of paper in his hand. He suspected that it may be the paper he signed when he handed over the money. What was he to say, he had to have an answer ready at the speed of lightning. Would they leave his family members alone, if he admitted delivering the money? He didn't want to involve his father and most of all his dear grandfather in this.

"I'm waiting… speak up."

"Yes, but…"

"No buts, do you admit handing over the money to them?"

"Yes, I do. We were threatened. Our lorries were burnt, one of them fell down a cliff. I was obliged to give them the money."

"So, you gave them the money?"

"Yes."

"Who gave it to you?"

"I took it from my father."

"So he knew all about it and offered you the money?"

"No, my father knew nothing of this. I didn't tell him why I wanted the money."

"So, why would he just hand over that amount of money to you?"

"I told my father that I had gambling debts to settle."

"Did he believe you?"

"Yes, he did."

"You don't say."

"Yes, you see, I had been in some trouble before because of my gambling…"

"Let me congratulate you, your father must be very proud of you. So tell me then, had you given them money before?"

"Of course not!"

"How am I to know you're telling me the truth?"

"You can check the names of the people I owed money to at the City Club..."

"Your word is my command," the commander said cynically.

"What I meant to say is that if you don't believe me and you felt you needed further proof..."

"If you tell me the truth, I don't need proof, I'll believe you. The guy you handed the money to, was one of the gamblers from the City Club, is that it?"

"No, I never gambled with him."

"One moment son. Are you now telling me, you took the money to the City Club?"

"No, not there."

"Where, then?"

"At... at the billiard saloon."

"Oh, at the billiard saloon."

"Yes."

"Why there?"

"So that, no one would see us, that's why."

"Do you mean to tell me that nobody saw you in that crowded place?"

"No, I handed it over in the lavatory."

"What was the name of the person you handed it over to?"

Cengiz tried to remember the name the guy in the duffle coat signed on the receipt and recalled it just in time.

"Well done, it's good of you to support the separatists. Tell me now who else do you know from this organisation?"

"Nobody."

"You're boring me now, Kasrıkoğlu. Are you going to spill the beans or shall we start? Believe you me, I have no intention of spending the day here trying to ease words out of your mouth."

"I swear, Sir, I don't know anyone else. Honest to God, I don't."

The Commander got up from his chair opposite Cengiz. He took a black cloth out of his pocket and tied it around Cengiz's eyes.

"Get up, dear Sir," he said, "I can see that we won't be able to settle this matter amicably."

Cengiz got up and the Commander man-handled him out into the corridor and after making him walk a short way, he pushed him into another room and made him sit on a chair without removing the blindfold. Cengiz realised that they were not alone because there were other voices in the room. He repeated the same answers to the same questions that he was asked time and time again. Yes, he had handed money over to the organisation to stop them burning their lorries and sending threatening letters. Yes, he had paid over the money in the hope that it would put an end to it. No, he wasn't a member of the organisation and he didn't know any of its members. No, he had no sympathy for their cause. He repeated the same answers over and over again. Finally, he got tired of these repeated questions being asked in different ways by the five different people and exploded.

"You're obviously trying to put words into my mouth but you won't succeed," he said. "I have nothing whatsoever to do with this organisation and know none of its members. I know no names and have no addresses. Whether you intend to keep me here for a month, a year or ten years, you will keep on getting the same answers, the truth. Please, either let me go or throw me into prison, but for God's sake stop asking me the same questions."

Someone slapped him viciously across the face causing him to fall to the floor. He lost consciousness while being kicked around.

The sound of terrifying wailing woke Cengiz from a deep sleep. It was a very strange sound, like the howling of a wounded animal. It was as if someone was ululating continuously, sometimes loudly and sometimes like mumbling and then suddenly very shrilly. Having been brought up on a farm, he was used to the screams of the women in labour and the howling of animals, but this was worse than that. He felt a sudden shudder and tried to work out where the noise was coming from. He tried to fathom out whether it was next door or downstairs to no avail. He was aching all over but when he became accustomed to the darkness he tried to get up, hit his head and fell back down. He raised his hands and then realised that he was lying on the bottom bunk which probably meant that he was not alone, this pleased him. He tried to remember how he got here, but the last memory he had was of being blindfolded and interrogated, the rest was blank… totally blank.

As the daylight filtered into the room, he could see that it was very narrow with several bunk beds. There was another person asleep on the top bunk across the room. Not only was there no other furniture in the room, but there were no mattresses either. Cengiz wound his fingers in the rough hair blanket he was lying on. He must have been lying on the iron bars of his bunk all night long causing him to ache all over or so he thought. He turned over on to his back, put his hands behind his head and tried to go back to sleep.

This time he was woken by the sound of something being thrown on to the floor from the door. There was a blood-stained man on the floor; the soles of his feet were swollen like loaves of bread fresh from the oven. His purple, bruised eyelids were so swollen, that he couldn't open his eyes. Blood was pouring from his nose and two of his fingers were hanging in their skin as if they had been broken. His trousers were wet and he stank of urine.

The man he thought was sleeping on the opposite bunk jumped to the floor and together he and Cengiz gently lifted the lump on to a bottom bunk. Cengiz took the blanket he was sleeping on and covered the trembling man.

"What's your name?" asked the man who had jumped from his bed.

"Cengiz… Cengiz Kasrıkoğlu."

"I'm Kadir."

Cengiz attempted to shake the man's hand but Kadir just nodded his head and put his right hand to his heart, Cengiz's hand was left in the air.

"Why are you here?" he asked the man.

"For treason, betraying my country, how about you?"

"The same."

"Did you really?"

"God forbid and you?"

"What a bloody country this is," said Kadir.

Cengiz thought to himself, that's all I needed. Realising that there was obviously no segregation between those who did and those who didn't love their country in this place, he decided not to get too involved with this stranger and went back to his bunk. He had to sit on the cold iron bars as he had given away his own blanket. A little while later he couldn't resist asking:

"Do you know this guy?"

"You mean Cafer, he's a traitor, too," Kadir replied, "just like us."

"I'm not a traitor."

"Doesn't make any fucking difference, mark my words, you'll be tortured anyway. Where did you say you came from?"

Cengiz told him the name of the city he came from.

"Oh! God! You're really in for it."

Cengiz was taken aback by the guy's bluntness. I hope you're wrong, you fucking son of a bitch, he thought to himself.

Half an hour later, the door opened clumsily and a soldier came in carrying a tray with three cups of tea and three slices of bread and put it down on the floor. As Cengiz reached for one of the cups, he was punched in the chest by the soldier.

"My, my, my, aren't we in a hurry!" he barked. "Are you very hungry?"

"Yes."

"Tell me first though, what's the first thing you say every morning?"

Cengiz looked very confused.

"Tell me you idiot!"

"Tell you what?"

"First you sing the National Anthem and then you recite the oath."

"Sing the National Anthem," said Kadir.

"I've got an awful voice."

"Get on with it you sissy or I'll make you sing it my way."

Cengiz stood to attention and was just about to start when the soldier interrupted him turning to Kadir.

"You, too, you fucking dog, get down here."

Kadir jumped to the floor and stood to attention with his arms stiffly by his sides.

"You, too, on the double!" he shouted at the wretched man lying like a corpse on the bed.

"He can't get up," said Cengiz. "Can't you see he's in no state to get up?"

"Hold your tonguc man, no one's asking you."

"They bought him in a while ago, he's passed out."

The soldier slapped Cengiz across the face and just as Cengiz was about to retaliate Kadir held his arms.

"He's a rookie alright, isn't he? Give him time, he'll learn," Kadir said trying to make light of the situation.

Cengiz pulled his arms away from Kadir.

The soldier who was obviously irritated by Cengiz's attitude shouted again, "If all three of you don't stand to attention right here in front of me, you know what I'm going to shove up your bloody arses, don't you?"

Kadir moved towards the man lying on the bunk and told Cengiz to help him. They held the poor wretch under each arm and managed to hold him upright, despite his sagging knees, by squeezing him between themselves. Together they started singing the National Anthem. Every time they made a mistake they were hit on the legs. After the Anthem they recited the Oath together. Finally, the ordeal was over and they carried the poor guy back to his bunk.

"He said nothing, so now you'll do it all again on his behalf," said the soldier.

Kadir and Cengiz stood side by side again and tried to do it all without making any mistakes. However, every time they did make a mistake they were hit on the legs with a stick and made to start from the beginning again. Eventually, when the soldier left, Cengiz dropped his trousers to examine his bruised legs. His bones were aching.

"Guys like him are beaten up by everyone from the day they're born to the day they wear the uniform," explained Kadir. "They're beaten by the mothers, their fathers, their uncles, the teachers at their schools and their landowners in the fields. Then, they're sent into the army and this time they're beaten up by their superiors. Do you know how? Well I'm sure you do… Then the moment they put on their bean green uniforms, suddenly, they feel they have the power to retaliate. They're full of their own importance and want to make sure they give as good as they got. For God's sake whatever you do make sure not to step on their toes!"

"I've got nothing to do with the soldiers, so why should I step on their toes?" Cengiz replied thinking to

himself what a know-all this Kadir is.

"You'll soon learn!"

Cengiz didn't respond and took a cup of tea from the tray. He took one sip and spat it out immediately. The tea had gone cold and as for the bread, God knows it was no different to yesterday's; he didn't even try it and put the tea back on the tray before returning to lie on the iron bars of his bunk. When the soldier returned a little while later he saw that Cengiz had not touched his food.

"What's wrong? I thought you were hungry," he said.

"The tea has gone cold and the bread is stale," replied Cengiz.

"What the fuck do you expect you little runt, five star service?"

"Please don't swear at me. I'm not complaining, I just don't want to eat it."

"You fucking poof. I think you need sorting out."

"Why? What have I done?"

"Aren't you one of these buggers who want to divide up our country? Isn't that enough, do you want me to go on?"

"I said no such thing."

"So, why are you here then?"

"I don't know, you'd better ask those that brought me here."

"I'm asking you!"

"Leave off!"

The soldier slapped Cengiz violently across the face and a fracas started before Kadir could intervene. Cengiz and the soldier were rolling all over the floor. Suddenly the soldier managed to free himself from Cengiz and darted straight for the door. When he returned a few minutes later, there were three other men with him. They got hold of Cengiz and dragged him out of the room. The sun was just rising in the sky.

Towards evening the cell door opened and there was Cengiz supported by two men. His nose was bleeding and there was blood all over his face. His pants were wet and reeked of urine and the seat of his trousers was ripped. Three of his fingers and his front teeth were broken and his eyes were swollen and totally closed up. The men pushed him in through the door. Cengiz fell into the middle of the floor like an empty sack.

***

Sadık Ağa had woken up at the sound of the first cockerel crowing. He was anxious to be ready for the District Governor's visit. He knew that he was coming to acknowledge his charitable donations. Fixing the school roof and providing an x-ray machine for the village clinic. He had instructed the women to prepare their finest pastries and cook their special dishes. The first thing he did when he got up was to go and collect the freshly laid eggs for the District Governor. He had shaved and chosen to wear his brown suit rather than his robes for this special occasion. His newly polished shoes and his watch chain across his waistcoat completed the picture. He was sitting under the pergola, cigarette in hand, trying to think of the best way to tackle the problem.

Had the Governor not expressed his desire to visit him, he would never have dreamt of asking for his help. Wouldn't he just? On second thought, yes, he would even if he had to drag his feet all the way to the Governor's office. Not only because the pain in his heart had stripped him of his dignity, but also because Dündar Leventoğlu was a district governor with very special qualities. As soon as he had taken up his post, he made a point of visiting every one of the villages and speaking to the landowners the headmen and muhtars and the village elders. He listened intently to all their problems and promised to do everything in his power to put them right. His first act was to create a Community Health Centre. Money contributed by wealthy people would be collected in one pot and distributed, according to needs by the donors themselves. As a sign of appreciation the donors would have each new installation named after them. Those who could not afford money gave of their time and skills. By doing this, the Governor managed to give start to all sort of projects. Schools were repaired and maintained, new equipment was purchased for the Health Centre, the roads were asphalted, vaccines were provided for the children and circumcisions for the boys. Leventoğlu was a very modest man, but he never passed up an invitation to attend a function if it would further his causes and strengthen his ties with the local people.

Sadık Ağa had realised that he could no longer bear the guilt of his burden alone. Sure he had thrown Cengiz into the fire, but now he needed someone to provide the tongs to get him out of it. If those tongs were to be provided by a kind-hearted person, he would appeal to their conscience but if they were to be provided by a mean person he would offer bribes. He was prepared to pull out all the stops to get his beloved grandson freed.

Taking a long drag on his cigarette, he thought to himself just how much easier it would have been if the District Governor were a money grabber even though, deep in his heart, he knew that this situation could not be solved with money. In fact, at this time, just after the military coup, it was difficult to appeal to people either via their consciences or their wallets. Maybe it would be best to tell the whole story just the way it is. He was curious to know if Cengiz had put himself in a compromising situation while he was under surveillance. How were they to know if they couldn't speak to the lad. They didn't even know where he was. Sadık Ağa sighed with despair. He threw his cigarette on the ground, held his hands open to God and started to pray. When he saw the dust disturbed by the jeep as it approached the farm, he ended his prayer with a quick 'Amen', stroked his face with his two hands and got up to greet the visitor. He walked towards the garden door through the pistachio trees.

It was a bright sunny day, the plum and apple trees were bursting into blossom and the air was filled with the scent of linden. Sadık Ağa's eldest daughter-in-law had done him proud by providing her best dishes for the Governor, the family entertained him beautifully. The conversation flowed easily over the long breakfast. The Governor explained that it was wrong to expect everything to be done by the government and many good things could be achieved if everybody chipped in. Sadık Ağa told anecdotes about his experiences with previous governors and when the goodies were eaten and the coffee drunk the other men left the room, as they had been instructed, leaving Sadık Ağa and the Governor alone together. Even though there was no one else in the room, Sadık Ağa preferred to be cautious and suggested that they retire to his own room. Once there, they sat side by side on the Ağa's comfortable divan.

The Ağa cleared his throat before speaking in a low voice.

"I'd like to ask a favour, Dündar Bey, if I may," he said. "I am asking you as a father not as the Governor. I will continue to support your worthy causes because I believe in them. But this favour I am about to ask is priceless and cannot be repaid by such material things."

"For God's sake, Sadık Ağa, what the hell is it that such an illustrious citizen as you who owns several villages can possibly need to ask of me?"

"I just told you, my dear sir, that the favour I will ask of you has nothing to do with money. You will have noticed that I have addressed you as a gentleman, not as a Governor, because this is not an official matter. It is something you might do only if you believe and trust me, not as a Governor but as another human being, as a father."

"Whatever is all this about?"

"It's a matter of life and death."

"Life and death?"

"That's right. It's about the fate of a young man, an innocent, blameless young man who has committed no crime but who has been sacrificed in my place. I'm even willing to offer my life in exchange for his. I wonder if it would be possible for them to exchange me for him, if they could set him free and take me instead."

"I don't understand what you're talking about. What exactly is it that you want from me?"

Sadık Ağa explained the whole story to the District Governor starting with the threatening letters and telling in detail everything that followed. He even went back as far as the Sheikh Said days to prove how faithful to the government his family had been. It was all in the archives if he needed any further assurances.

"I know you very well, I don't need any assurances, Sadık Ağa," the Governor said. "It's very clear to me that young Cengiz is innocent and is suffering because of a wrong decision made by you."

"You're right, it was wrong of me to send him with the money."

"No, it was wrong of you not to have informed the police when you were first threatened. I wish you could have trapped the robbers while delivering the money. Not only would you not be in this situation right now, but you would also have helped the authorities catch them red-handed."

"You're right, so very right. I made a mistake but I don't want my grandson to suffer the consequences of it. Do you think you can help?"

"First of all we have to find out where he is. Pray to God that he is still alive, otherwise what good will my help do? Let's first find out if he's alive and if so where he is."

There was a knock on the door and a young girl of about ten entered carrying two frothy ayrans on a tray. She was followed by a younger little girl with beautiful dark eyes. The older one placed the tray on a table in front of the divan.

"These are my grand-daughters," said the Ağa. "They are both orphans. As you know, life is very cheap hereabouts. This family of mine has lost many members throughout the years. Some were killed during tribal disputes or family feuds others in traffic accidents. I don't want to experience any more of this pain. Enough is enough! If you should find my beloved Cengiz and help us save him, I will be eternally grateful to you. I shall owe you my life."

"No, I don't want you to owe me anything, Sadık Ağa. I'll do my best to find out where they have taken your grandson. Not only because I know you are telling me the truth but also because his name is Cengiz."

"Don't tell me your father's name was Cengiz, too!"

"No, it was the name I had given to my still-born son. I had named him after my best friend in the army during my military service."

"May he rest in peace. *Inshallah*, God will give you many more sons."

After picking up the empty mugs the two little girls left the room. The Governor stood up and shook hands with Sadık Ağa. The old man pressed the Governor's hand between his and seemed to want to say something but a lump stuck in his throat and he said nothing. The two men spoke with their eyes. The Governor's clear look said, "I'm going to do everything I can," and the Ağa's sad, tear-filled eyes said, "God bless you."

***

Cengiz had finally forgotten how many days he had been here. Was it ten days? Twenty? Or had he been sleeping for months in this narrow airless cell? It was as if time had lost its meaning and the hope that he was clinging to so tightly was slipping away. His life now had a new routine. He had to stand to attention first thing in the morning and sing the National Anthem before reciting, at the top of his voice, the Oath. Needless to say if he made any mistakes while doing so there were the beatings to be endured. Of course, there was also the terrible soup and stale bread to swallow if he wanted to survive. The worse thing was the lavatories; they were blocked most of the time and it was his duty, on alternate days, to clean the disgusting mess. Other prisoners came and went. Exercise consisted of being taken out into the yard as a chain gang to get some fresh air and once a week they would try to take a shower under ice-cold drops of water. As soon as the sun went down they were made to sleep in their bunks. It was forbidden to talk to each other after lights out. Furthermore, it was also forbidden to complain, anyone who did was doused with a hose and then beaten, if they should dare to ask a question, the reply was always the same, abuse followed by a thrashing or even torture depending on their reaction.

An elderly man who had been interrogated and tortured was lying in his bunk when the soldier came in for the morning rituals. When the old man did not respond to his orders the soldier grabbed the thin mattress the man was laying on and threw it to the middle of the cell. The old man's body fell out of the mattress and rolled to the feet of the other five prisoners who were standing to attention.

"Oh my God! He's dead," one of them exclaimed.

Immediately, Kadir rushed to the old man's bunk and moved his blanket into his own. That sickened Cengiz.

"You crafty bugger," shouted the soldier even though he hadn't stopped Kadir taking the blanket.

"What do you expect? My back is beginning to look as if I'm lying on a fire grid. Unless I'm mistaken, I am the most senior prisoner in this cell so…"

"Shut up you cheeky sod! Get back in line before I kick your arse. All of you remain at attention until I get back."

The soldier was obviously going to get some help to remove the corpse. Cengiz looked at the poor man lying at his feet and saw that after so many days of torment, he was finally at peace. Cengiz realised that from now on his priority must be to get out of this place, dead or alive, there was no longer any point in him trying to prove his innocence. He should escape or die!

Cengiz was finally located nearly five months after his disappearance. He was found at the Military Headquarters where prisoners were held for interrogation prior to their trials. His trial date was moved forward as a result of the Governor's intervention. The Governor persistent protestations of his innocence led him to be cleared of all charges and sent back to his village. His father carried him carefully through the autumn leaves that were covering the ground, into the farm. Even his own mother didn't recognise him. He had lost nine kilos and his jet black hair had turned grey. He couldn't bend the fingers of his left hand and his front teeth were missing. His eyes had sunk back into their sockets. The stinging pain and hate in his eyes produced such a chilling effect that it was impossible to believe how young he really was.

NEVRA and ZELHA

Tears were running down my face. I pressed the stop button on the tape-recorder in front of Zelha.

"You're a bit late for that," Zelha said to me. "The tape ran out ages ago; didn't you notice?"

"Why didn't you tell me? I could have put another one in."

"What for? I'm sure you won't want to listen to all that again, now that you've got the answer to your question."

"True, I did, there's something to learn every day, but do I ever learn? Look, for instance you noticed that the tape had run out and I didn't. A bit like my life really, the empty spool goes on turning and I am not aware of it. I keep on waiting in hope. I'm always waiting in vain for something to happen."

"Here, take this and blow your nose." Zelha passed one of the paper napkins to me and I blew my nose.

"Come on now, enough tears, it's no use crying over spilt milk, what has happened has happened."

"But I wish it hadn't."

"I no longer cry over anything. I've become as hard as nails."

There was a lump in my throat and I couldn't manage to clear it. I was just sitting there without finding anything to say. I didn't know who I should feel sorry for; Cengiz, my father, Dede or the Kurdish and Turkish youngsters dying in the mountains. Who should I blame for bringing this paradise of a country of ours to this dreadful situation? Is there no way other than using violence and torture to solve the problems. Should I lay blame he politician, the nationalist, the army, the tradesman, the imams or the fundamentalists? Who? Who?

I felt crushed inside. I didn't know if it was because I was hungry or because of all that brutality. I rummage in my bag and got the apples. I gave one to Zelha. She took it and immediately bites into it, I bited on mine too and the juice ran from the side of my mouth. It took me back to those beautiful apple trees covered in full blossom looking like young brides dressed for their weddings. As kids Zelha and I would pick the young blossoms and make crowns of them. I well remember the joy we got out of wearing them and running around the farm shouting, 'Look at us! Be have become brides! We've become brides!' What else could we have wished for at that age and on that farm? We used to dream of having a joint wedding where we would both be wearing apple blossom head-dresses. Then we would live near one another in big houses with big gardens full of apple and cherry trees. Each of us would have two sons and two daughters and they would all grow up together and marry each other. In that way we would become genuine relatives and we would never part.

But we grew up and our ways did part. Both our gardens and our worlds separated. We each got married far away from the other and in different cities without an apple blossom head-dress in sight. Instead we wore crowns of sorrow which we didn't deserve and far from becoming relatives, we almost became enemies. Oh, dear Zelha, why on earth did all this happen?

While listening to my dear friend I realised that I have been comparatively luckier than her. I felt strangely guilty deep in my heart. I was a city girl after all and have no right to complain. I don't know what it was like to have a kuma, what it was to be arrested, imprisoned and tortured. I have never been involved in a blood feud either. I was just grieved by all the horror stories I heard. I felt as though the more questions I ask and the more I listen to Zelo's answers, the more I may be able to understand the pains she suffered.

"Tell me. Zelha, did you see Cengiz after he returned home?"

"Of course I did, he never went back to the city after that, he stayed right in the village."

"How come I have never seen him then?"

"He never came out to mix with people. Frankly he was quite weird… Of course, in those days, I knew nothing of what he had been through, I just thought he was a bit nutty like Sülü."

"Odd that with all my comings and goings to and from the farm I never came across him."

"Well as I just said, he never used to speak to anyone or mix with visitors. That's why my dear old grandmother kept asking the imams to come to the house to pray for him. Not only that, but because she believed in old wives tales, she would ask those who claimed to be able to exorcise evil spirits to prepare special charms for her grandson. Sadly nothing worked for poor Cengiz. I do remember him coming out once when your father visited the farm… but… never mind."

"What do you mean, never mind! Tell me what happened."

"I said never mind!"

"Absolutely no, Zelha. Please finish what you have started… What did he do when my father visited the farm? Did he come out to thank him?"

"That's what my grandfather and uncle thought… They thought he wanted to express his gratitude for being saved; they imagined that he wanted to kiss your father's hand or something."

"My father never liked people kissing his hands."

"Don't worry, he didn't. He said he was sorry that your father had found and saved him. He said that he wished he had been left to die there. 'Look at me,' he said, 'I have no soul, no pride nor any reason to live. I'm nothing Officer,' he shouted at your father. 'There's nothing left of me, absolutely nothing!' Then he did something very shameful… I remember my grandfather was furious…"

"What did he do?"

Zelha kept quiet.

"For God's sake, Zelha, what did he do?"

"He spat."

"Spat? At my father?"

"No, on the floor."

"And what did my father do?"

"Apparently he said, 'I kept my promise to you Sadık Ağa. I found your grandson and had him returned to you. The rest is up to you. You must find a way to bring him back to life.' Then he got up and left."

"What a shame, I don't think my father deserved that."

"Not at all but then Cengiz was not himself any more... He was insane."

"Did he ever come to his senses?"

"He stayed on the farm for quite some time not going anywhere, not even to the dentist. He saw nobody. He just sat there for hours with his eyes fixed on the wall. People who wanted to keep him company came and went; in fact, if Dede was around he wouldn't allow them to bother him. And then what do you think happened, Nevo?"

"What?"

"He ran away to join the rebels in the mountains."

"Oh no, after all that."

"You can say that again."

"Did you see him any more?"

"Yes, we did. He visited the farm a few times, secretly of course. Every time he came, Dede tried to persuade him to turn himself in. You might remember, from time to time the government would declare an amnesty for the rebels who were prepared to give themselves in. Poor old Dede kept on sending him messages every time there was a pardon. Then, once, right after Cengiz had visited the farm we were raided and they searched everywhere thoroughly. That was it, we never saw Cengiz after that."

"I now realise why my father had fallen from grace, Zelo."

"What do you mean?"

"Well, can you imagine? It was my father who found Cengiz and got him released from prison and then he goes and joins the rebels. I mean… how do you think that reflected on my father? That put the lid on him every becoming a Governor General."

"Don't tell me your poor father never became a Governor General?"

"No, he was posted to Urla yet again as a District General and that did it. He applied for early retirement… on medical grounds."

"I'm so sorry, Nevo. No wonder Dede kept on warning Cengiz, after he had run away, that he could cause some people a lot of trouble."

"Yes indeed, Zelo. Terrorism has really put a lot of people in trouble."

"But, on the other hand, Nevo, do you think people turned to terrorism willingly; on the spur of the moment they pick up their bags and move to the mountains to indulge in a little killing sport? Is that what you really think?"

"I know that certain people have to do certain things to get their message across, but I'm also sure that they could have got to this point without all that bloodshed. It might have taken a little longer, that's all."

"Do you really believe in what you're saying?"

"Of course. For God's sake, Zelo, just what has been achieved as a result of all that bloodshed? What actual gains have been made? Thousands of dead and wounded people, loads of bitter memories, that's all. The world is changing very rapidly, my love, and people, nations and religions who can't keep up with those changes will find that they have no place in this new world. Violence and bloodshed will achieve nothing, what is needed is dialogue, compromise and reconciliation before a solution can be found."

"You wouldn't be talking like this if you had seen Cengiz when he returned to the farm. He was no longer a human being. He was gutted. He could neither sleep nor eat. This man who wouldn't even harm a fly was overcome by rage. He couldn't find what he wanted with us. He couldn't wait for the changes you talk about. He went seeking revenge and retaliation. You keep saying that bloodshed is wrong but isn't turning a person into a monster just as wrong?"

"You're right, it is. But don't forget Zelha... Both sides are responsible for creating these monsters... In my opinion both sides are continuously fanning the same fire. The whole bloody issue has turned into a vendetta. Can't you see that all this 'you and us' is causing more pain and sorrow? I'd love to know how much longer it will take you to realise that a sensible solution is better than an impossible one. Luckily, right now, we have a government that believes in reconciliation. If there is more bloodshed the people will get all worked up and vote for the power which advocates tougher measures. If that happens, we'll all suffer the consequences. The Cengizes of this world need to climb down the mountains, Zelo, and join us. It's absolutely necessary..."

"It's too late for our Cengiz to climb down, he will stay there forever."

"Why?"

"Because... because he's dead, that's why. He was shot!"

Words get stuck in my throat and I look at Zelo like the village idiot.

"We haven't even got a grave that we can visit because his body was never recovered. Our lots seem to have disposed of the corpse before the soldiers came for it. Dede was hysterical. Night after night he went around the gardens like a wounded bull, yelling at the trees, the mountains and the stars for months on end. Eventually, he fell into his bed delirious with fever. He never recovered. The poor man disintegrated before his time. He became a bent-up old man showing no interest in anything and never stepping out of the farm. Even as he drew his last breath he was mumbling Cengiz's name. So there you have it, Nevo!"

***

Zelha said 'our lot'… I wonder who 'our lot' is. Who are those people who removed Cengiz's body before it could be laid to rest in a marked grave for his family to remember him by? And what about Dede himself; that darling cuddly Dede who used to rock me to sleep on his lap. Would he be considered one of us or one of them? Who are we? Who are they? Look at us right now one woman from us and one from them sitting opposite one another and crying. The pain in one heart was hurting the other. I don't know what sort of expression there is on my face, but together with the uncontrollable shaking of my body, it must have been relaying to Zelha the revulsion that I was feeling.

She spoke reassuringly to me, "It's not your fault," she said. "Don't look at me with such shame in your eyes but, do me a favour and stop trying to convince me of this, that and the other. I have no time for all of that. I'm totally distraught, I'm devastated… Let's just leave it at that!"

I feel devastated, too. Those I love as well have also been scattered all over the place let alone the suffering they had to endure. Just look at my poor father. Who knows how many times he had to defend himself at the Ministry of the Interior for his humane actions toward another human being. How was he to know that it would eventually reflect on his future within the service? He never got the promotion he so rightly deserved. Did he know that a once decent young man could be turned into a monster by a few maniacs? Unlike my mother, he never expressed his feelings but he must have been really hurt by the whole affair; he considered it undignified to discuss his disappointment. I believe that he was caught between a rock and a hard place. On the one hand, the Government because of the Cengiz business and, on the other, my mother. If I, as their child, was so wounded by her departure who knows how he must have suffered. How quietly he buried his shame and pain. He neither challenged his wife nor his superiors; instead he chose to opt out altogether and retire to a fishing village and spend his days fishing. If he were to be aware of my thoughts, I'm absolutely sure that he would defend the government. He would say, 'How on earth could they appreciate my interference on behalf of someone who turned out to be a rebel? The State has to defend and protect itself. One of the many duties our army has alongside protecting our borders is to defend our principles,' or words to that effect.

He was from another generation, nowadays we expect our army to simply protect our borders. I presume that this generation must be a bad vintage because according to us, to love our country had taken on a different meaning. My brother, for instance, despite being brought up with a father totally devoted to his country, did not want to live here. I would imagine my brother must have sensed my father's bottled up emotions when he deciding to settle in America;

"What good can I expect from those who didn't appreciate my father's worth? I'm not an idealist patriot like him imbued with tolerance and devotion. I'd like to try my luck in a country where human values are appreciated."

"But you're not a public servant, Orhan," I had said. "You're going to be a scientist, that's nothing to do with politics. Please don't go."

"You'd better come and have a look at the state of the university," he had said. "Universities are supposed to be seats of learning but nowadays if it's learning you want, they hate you. As long as you're a narrow minded bigot who's happy to leave things as they are, then you are OK. Sorry, that's not for me."

"This country needs people like you," I pleaded. "Otherwise we are doomed to stay just as we are without making any progress."

"I'm sorry to say that this country is doomed to stay just the way it is because it is ruled by mediocre people without a vision. I'm a scientist, Nevra; I can't bear mediocrity and stagnant people. Unchanging situations would stifle me."

While terror kept killing people, unchanging stagnant situations killed people's souls.

What terrible times we have lived through. As if death on the fields, death in the mountains, death in the cities were not enough, narrow mentalities killed intelligent peoples' souls. Stubbornness on both sides has meant that a political solution would not be found to stop young men from dying. Mothers left grieving for their sons, wives left grieving for their husbands, children left fatherless. I, too, had quite a number of stories to tell Zelo on the subject. Maybe I haven't lost any relatives but all the same, is it possible not to be effected by that silent war?

It's almost four years ago now, my neighbour Ferhunde's son had been doing his military service in the East. Ferhunde was a very kind lady much loved by all her neighbours. Whenever she'd cooked savoury pastries or cabbage leaf dolmas she'd knock on my door with a plate full of them, saying that as a working girl I did not have time for such time consuming dishes, so she had spared me a plate.

I tried to reciprocate by bringing her magazines from the office. She was extremely distraught to learn that her son had been wounded, yet happy that he would be discharged and send home. A day before his arrival, the poor woman cooked enough food to feed an army. She cleaned and tidied every corner of her flat, then went out to rent one of those adjustable orthopaedic beds. I prepared a sign at work saying 'WELCOME HOME OUR BRAVE WAR HERO' which we hung over the gate of our complex. With the help of all the neighbours, we decorated the entrance to our block with flowers and waited there all together to greet him. Finally a military vehicle pulled up outside. A soldier jumped out and ran to the back of the vehicle. He reached inside and lifted out what looked like a big child in his arms. I saw Ferhunde and her daughter Nevin rush forward to the vehicle but suddenly Ferhunde's legs buckled under her, Nevin tried to support her but they both fell slowly to the ground like a film in slow motion.

My God! My God! Was that bundle in the soldier's arms our tall, goodlooking Tamer? Ferhunde's one and only son! My stomach comes up into my mouth and my legs are shaking. I stagger inside and throw myself into an armchair. I pray to God that what I had seen was a figment of my imagination… Please God let it not be true. I had to pull myself together to go and visit the family, to say 'Welcome home, Tamer.'

Can I bear to look Ferhunde straight in the face?

What shall I say?

'Don't worry my dear, your son is back home now, safe and sound, it could have been much worse you know… God has spared him for you. Just imagine, if one of the terrorist's mines exploded under him and killed him!' Is that what I'm supposed to say to console her?

Tamer had finished university as the top student of his year. He had gone to do his military service as soon as he graduated, a typical young man of twenty-three, he was engaged and looking forward to getting married when he returned. Yes, that was our handsome Tamer with a brilliant future ahead of him! Now... he had no legs.

Those who influenced Zelha and who thought that terrorism was the only way to fight their cause, are responsible for the young men left limbless, hopeless and miserable. They have turned some people, like Dede's grandson Cengiz, into both victim and killer and others into drug addicts...

How is Zelha to know that a colleague of mine, who had witnessed some atrocious scenes during a raid, has to take handfuls of pills every night so that he can sleep and not relive every dreadful moment of that experience? He was just an innocent bystander with not a thought of shooting or killing anyone in his head.

As a keen new journalist eager to prove my worth I threw myself into every project that came my way. On one such occasion I found myself in a village near Erzincan. My boss had instructed me to write an emotional article from a woman's point of view; he didn't want a run of the mill report on a raid. All the way there I kept on thinking about how I was going to approach this assignment. How did a woman's feelings differ from a man's when it came to death and violence?

It was a difficult journey there in those days; before the bridge was built over the Fırat river.

The terrorists had travelled overnight through the mountains and rounded all the inhabitants up in the village square. They had lined all the men up alongside the mosque wall and machine-gunned them in the head. Then, they burnt all the village houses. A bed-ridden old woman was turned to charcoal in her bed. The Governor at the time decreed that, because of the extreme summer heat, all the corpses would be buried immediately before their relatives could see what had been done to them thus avoiding an escalation of the situation.

Our photographer Erkal had been able to capture in his pictures the horror and pain in the faces of the wives and children of the thirty-three men who had been shot. Needless to say, he had also managed to photograph the remains of the houses and the ruined village.

That same evening, at a hotel in the city, one of the local journalists had secretly shown Erkal photographs he had taken of the corpses laid out side by side before they were buried. Erkal was sitting next to me. His face had turned as white as a sheet and he wasn't even aware that he had retched while looking through the photographs. I tried to reach one of the photographs to look at it myself but he rudely pushed me away causing me to nearly fall off my chair.

"Get off! Don't you dare look at them!"

I let go of the corner of the photograph I had managed to reach.

"For God's sake, Nevra, leave off, this is not for you… These bodies have… no… no faces… no heads."

"OK. I understand, point taken. Don't tell me any more."

Erkal's hands were trembling. He had immediately jumped up and run to the lavatory where he vomited. With the stench of burnt flesh in his nostrils and the sight of those photographs in his head, he was not able to sleep that evening without the aid of sleeping pills. As for me, I just don't know how I managed to sit in front of my typewriter throughout the night and produce the article my boss wanted, but I did and he congratulated me for it.

In those days of course I didn't know that the people I called terrorists were in fact Zelha's heroes. Just as I didn't know what had been done to Zelha's nephew by my heroes. In other words, there is no difference between us when it comes to cruelty. These methods inflicted to the enemy were destroying people both mentally and physically on both sides. Why couldn't our people change themselves? Why couldn't they try to see things from a different angle? And yet how alike we were in our stubbornness. How similar were our ways of expressing our anger and prove ourselves right.

***

I had so many stories I could tell Zelha but I didn't because I'm sure she'd had to live through enough stories of her own. She was sitting opposite me with a very sad expression on her face and resting her head in her hands.

"Have you got a headache, Zelo?" I asked.

"No... Do you know, Nevo, I suddenly feel very sorry for what happened to your dear father. Who knows what he had to undertake because of Cengiz? Who knows how many interrogations he had to endure? Who knows how unjustly he was treated?"

"A lot of water has gone under the bridge since then, Zelo, don't worry... He has a very peaceful life now. He's fine, he reads a lot, enjoys fishing and my son spends time with him during his summer holidays."

"All the same... when you think of it..."

"Yes, I'm sure he must have suffered but he never spoke about it though. It's understandable if the man he saved ended up being a terrorist... Bad luck, that's all."

"Who knows how he must have been disappointed in Cengiz? How much he must have cursed him?"

"I don't think so, Zelo. After all he wouldn't have insisted on calling my son Cengiz if he had, would he?"

"Oh yes, that's right; you told me about that."

"It was you who told me, have you forgotten? And... what's more, isn't it strange that it's still crystal clear in my memory... when he held my son in his arms for the first time he had said, 'I hope this Cengiz has a better life than the others, please god he makes a better job of his life. I wish him all the happiness and success in the world... may you always be proud of him.' I hadn't really understood what he meant at the time… poor father… how could I have known?"

"I, too, hope that your Cengiz will have all the luck the others didn't," said Zelo as a tear ran down her cheek.

"I thought there were to be no more tears," I said laughing.

"These are tears of hope and good will to wish your Cengiz all the very best."

"And for your children too. *Inshallah*, they'll all lead happy and healthy lives."

"*Inshallah.*"

"I am sure you agree, Zelo, that their happiness depends largely upon us."

"If only it were that simple… don't forget there are others than just us."

"But these others are also human beings after all. They might well have their own evaluation of the situation, but they're not Gods, are they? Now that everyone is waiting for your next move, please act courageously and according to your heart. Don't allow them to use you as a pawn in their game."

"I beg your pardon, what do you mean by that, Nevo?"

"I'm saying that you should put your foot down about what you consider to be right. Our generation may have lost the round, but the game's not over yet. There's still hope for our children, that they might live peacefully together as one nation. Please resist moves that you think wrong, don't allow them to use you to achieve their impossible dreams."

"I suppose, I'll always be that silly little weak tribe girl in your eyes. You just can't believe that I have a mind of my own, can you?"

"I'm so sorry that you misunderstood me, Zelha… Anyway… I have never thought of you as being weak since that day when we first met. You have always been quite an individual. Wasn't it you who always had her own way when we were kids?"

"We have a saying, Nevo, 'Every cock crows best in his own backyard'. Back in the village, maybe."

"Come on, wasn't it you who was doing all the crowing in our home, too? Or have you forgotten?"

"Ah, but I was taller than you then, not like now, look at you, you've grown so tall."

"So if it depends upon who's the tallest, it's now your turn to listen to me."

"But I'm still the eldest by about two years, Nevo."

She was right. They hadn't sent her to school when they should have done so, she was just over eight when we both went into the first form together. Most of the kids in the class were older than me anyway. I particularly remember a certain Baran who towered over us all. His grandfather had kept him in the fields to work, so his father was only able to send him to school after the old man had died.

"Do you remember Baran," I asked Zelo. "You might remember his nick-name, Baro the Pole because of his height.

Of course, she did. In fact she seemed to know an awful lot about him. Apparently, he had gone on to university, studied law and qualified as a solicitor. However, he didn't follow that through, instead, he became a rich businessman and earned a hell of a lot of money.

Every time we reached a stalemate in our political discussions, we both skilfully turned to the subject of the old days in Sarıcadam immediately easing the tension. That's exactly what we had done by talking about Baran and other school friends. Some had become members of the Parliament, lawyers and doctors. Others ended up becoming good for nothing or terrorists. Berfin was the only girl who had managed to complete her studies with a degree and became the village mid-wife, a job she was still doing to this day. She had fallen in love with a young doctor who was working at the village Health Clinic and they had got married and had three children. Apparently her aim was to teach all the village women about birth control. Most of the women secretly took precautions now without their husbands' knowledge. It seems the husbands were generally confused as to why suddenly the average family had four or five children when previously it had been nine or ten. They had no idea that Berfin had anything at all to do with it.

Time was running out, we had to part in about an hour. Maybe that's why we were avoiding political issues that we would never agree upon now and preferred to talk about the old days in the village. Oh dear! We had such fun, we certainly laughed a lot... We didn't realise how quickly time had flown by while we were chatting away. Then, as if tempted by the devil, I asked her about the young girls in the East. Those who were prevented from going to school and virtually kept as prisoners in their own homes by their fathers, uncles and particularly by their macho elder brothers keen to show their power over them. And then I poured salt on the wound by suggesting that, since she wasn't keen on the political side of things, she should concentrate her efforts on this issue. Wouldn't that be of more use to her people in the long run?

Zelha was obviously disappointed in me and looked me straight in the eyes saying, "I know exactly what you're trying to do Nevra Tuna! You foolishly think you can manipulate me by appealing to my soft sensitive side but what you are doing is making a bad joke of my being in prison. You think that you are the only person in the world who has presented me with the realities of today trying to persuade me to change my objectives. I can't believe that you can be so openly manipulative."

She was addressing me as Nevra Tuna for the first time since I introduced myself to her. I had certainly offended my friend which was not my intention. She reacted as if I had stabbed her with a knife. I jumped out of my seat and rushed to her side.

"Zelo, believe me as far as I'm concerned your being here in prison is a bad joke in itself... How can you imagine that I was trying to get the upper hand with a pack of nonsense?"

"Don't you worry your head about those girls. They are my girls, my people. Believe me they are more of a concern to me than they could ever be to you."

"Sure they speak your language but they are my fellow citizens, too. They're people of my motherland. Of course I have the right to worry about their predicament."

"Instead of just worrying, you should do something positive about it."

"Isn't that exactly what I am saying? We must all look out for them. As long as those girls in the East have no sense of identity and cannot live their lives like the rest of us, you, me and everybody else will be to blame because of our apathy. Mark my words!"

"I do."

"So, why don't you consider those girls as a priority? Leave everything else aside and concentrate on them."

"I've got to get out of here first."

"Why wait? You could start from right here. You could initiate a campaign for them to be educated."

"Going to school isn't their only problem."

"But without knowledge, how can they be expected to sort out their other problems. They have no idea what they are missing without education. For God's sake tell me, what can be achieved by these women when most of them are kept ignorant?"

"Shut up, Nevo! Don't be such a smart arse!"

"I'm not! I'm merely trying to underline the situation."

"And what's that exactly?"

"You, yourself! Don't you realise that you're beginning to turn into a mascot... a symbol if you like? Don't try to tell me you're not because I won't believe you."

"I'm not saying anything of the sort."

"Good, so in that case listen to me; since you're very well known these days, why can't you set an example to the girls from your borough?"

"Me, an example?"

"Why not, Zelo? With your personality, stature and political identity, you could do a hell of a lot. You could drop everything in hand, turn the page and try to do something about the oppressed women in the East. Be their role model and save them both from the men who dominate them and from ignorance."

"Are you suggesting that Turkish women are not oppressed?"

"Not at all, of course they are. Local customs and traditions still have a hold on them, too."

"There you are. So, why don't you try to save your own women?"

"I am trying to do just that but without segregation. I'm trying to do what I can for all young girls already. This has become a priority with me since the paper sent me to the East to report on the women out there."

"Haven't you missed the boat already?"

"Maybe I have but I have finally woken up."

"This is not a new problem you know, it has existed for centuries."

"Zelo, I'm not contradicting you I'm simply saying that I have only just woken up to it. Better late than never, isn't that so?"

"And you'll solve all the problems with an article in your newspaper? Well done, Nevo!"

"You can make fun of me as much as you like."

"Can you let me have a copy of this famous article of yours? I'd love to see how this enthusiasm manifests itself."

"It's not only my article... Something else happened which made me very sensitive to this subject."

"What was that?"

"Apparently, there's an association that offers scholarships to destitute young girls living in the rural parts of the East so that they can go to school... Have you heard about this?"

"I have, so what?"

"Well you see, last year I did a series of interviews with the girls who had taken up the offer of these scholarships. I had visited about fifty homes to interview them. Believe me, Zelo; it really highlighted the plight of these uneducated girls for me."

"You don't say!"

"Yes, I do. Maybe being banged up in here you were not aware of this. To be honest, I wasn't until I went to talk to them in their homes and saw first hand what a state they were in."

"How did you talk to them? Parrot fashion?"

"Don't be sarcastic. I spoke to them through an interpreter of course… I couldn't believe my eyes… the destitution… the desperation. We were pushed from pillar to post during the interviews. I was totally shocked when I realised that their lives consisted only of the home, the field and back to the home."

"This is incredible, Nevo. You're talking as if you had never seen Easter women before."

"As far as Eastern women are concerned, I've only met the women of your tribe. What I didn't know was that, in comparison to the others, women in your farm lived like queens, I can assure you! They always had food to eat, clothes on their backs, had their share of fun and laughter. Some of them even had the guts to give their men folk a taste of their own medicine, your grandmother for instance. You should have seen some of those women I saw in those hovels bringing up nine or ten children and already old by the time they were thirty."

"Do you think I haven't?"

"If you have then you can only agree with me. Destitution is a horrible thing, it's worse than ignorance. You'd never believe me if I told you the dreadful things I experienced."

"Try me, Professor!"

This time it was my turn to relate exactly what I saw and experienced in the God forsaken remote villages near Kars, Erzurum and Doğubeyazıt. I told her about Emine in Urfa whose father was ashamed to go to the coffee house because his daughter was the first and only girl who attended the lycee, about Ayşe, the orphan, who was sacked from her grandmother's house because she wanted to train as a nurse, about the children who had to walk five or ten kilometres a day in the snow and cold wearing only hand knitted sweaters and worn out shoes with holes on the soles and about Pınar from a mountain village who had to wait for at least half an hour for transport every morning, under heavy snow.

I told Zelha that I had warned her one extremely cold day that she would freeze if she didn't go back home. Surely buses wouldn't be running in such conditions. Her cheeks were crimson and her fingertips had turned mauve.

'I'm sure it will, come. Please don't worry,' she had said. 'That's how I go to school every day.' Can you imagine Zelo, a forty kilometre round trip between home and school every day? She was almost freezing and yet her eyes were smiling. Do you know why? Because she was going to school. There she was finally after centuries, doing something at last that could change her destiny. School was hope for her, her only hope."

"Unfortunately, that's the way it is out there. Even if families do want to send their children to school, the weather conditions and the terribly long journeys make it very difficult for them."

"The tribal laws are even worse than the weather conditions. Just think about all those women and young covered from head to toe in black. They're girls not allowed to go out in the daylight; they can't express their opinions or their feelings. All this because of ignorance and bigotry in those areas."

Zelha didn't make any comment. Even all those years ago the women of her tribe that I knew lived in much better conditions than the women I had met over the past few years. But Zelha knew exactly what I'm talking about.

"Just think, Zelo, I reckon that each family must have had about ten children. Some women gave birth to as many as fifteen. Their living areas were not as large as yours at the farm. They lived one on top of another in the tiniest of rooms. The houses were in such poor condition that snow fell indoors through the holes in the roof. I remember the pots and pans squeezed between the beds to catch the drips as the snow melted all over the place. There was something else that really hurt me. I came across a handicapped child in one out of two of the houses."

"Does that surprise you? Do you know why?"

"Of course I do. It's to be expected if a woman gives birth to so many babies; eventually one is going to be handicapped, isn't it? Then, of course, when she can no longer produce, in walks the Kuma! A new factory for a new production line... and then when faulty goods appear on the conveyor belt yet another Kuma comes along."

"Calm down, Nevo. Don't get so agitated. Your eyes are like daggers."

"Do you blame me? I wish I hadn't brought this subject up. I don't know why I did."

"Why then?"

"Because it's my pet aversion. Once I start on the subject, there's no stopping me. I'm sorry."

"There's nothing to apologise for. Don't forget I know about all of this anyway. Don't think I've only seen my father's and my husband's homes. I have visited quite a few other places in my capacity as a member of Parliament."

"In that case, there's no need for me to go on about it. You'll understand exactly how I feel."

"Of course I do. We had toilets built next to the houses in my husband Siyar's village but would they use them for the purpose intended? No they would not. They used them as sheds for the animals and insisted on walking to the stream whether it was a freezing cold winter or a boiling hot summer. I used to wonder if their bums froze in the winter."

We started laughing again. In fact this is what Zelha used to do when we were kids as well; whenever we had talked about something serious or argued with each other she'd immediately find the funny side of the story and that would be the end of our disagreement, but this time I didn't want to let go.

"Oh, Zelo! Toilets are nothing compared to some of the things that really annoy me. For instance, the mothers who don't stand up to their in-laws when their own daughter's lives are in jeopardy, or those women who turn a blind eye when some of the perverted men force their sisters- in-law, their sisters and even their own daughters to have sex with them. I really cannot stand that."

"Don't be unfair to those women, Nevo. Do you think they turn a blind eye because they want to? Not at all, if they uttered a single word they'd be killed instantly and it would be put down as a suicide or whatever..."

I continued to tell about those husbands who severely beat their wives often leaving them toothless. They had so many children that they couldn't look after them and feed them properly because they didn't want to know about birth control.

Zelha continued to listen to my tales, sometimes with tears in her eyes sometimes just wrapped in total concentration. I told her about all those cases of destitution, ignorance, injustice and misery. I was sure she was thanking her lucky stars that she did not have to endure such a life; just as I did when she told me her story.

"There's only one way to solve all this, Zelo. I firmly believe that there's only one solution to this problem."

"What's that? An earthquake which'll raze everything to the ground?"

"No, educate the girls."

"And I thought you'd say something different."

"No, I believe it's the only solution. Unless every woman in the East is made aware that the life she leads is not a life but hell on earth..."

"Do you think that's easy?"

"No, but it's possible."

"With education?"

"Yes."

"My darling old friend, my well meaning, gullible old friend."

"Don't say that, Zelo. After all we're the self same people who went through the War of Liberation and who got rid of the French, Italians and British who looked down on us, aren't we?"

"Believe me, that was an easier task. We can do it again if they should dare to return. We know how to fight. What we don't know is how to be human beings."

"There's still hope as long as we get our priorities right and educate our girls. Make them aware of what life is really about."

"What about the men?"

"The more educated and knowledgeable the girls become, the more the men will change, too."

"Dream on, Nevo. Dream on!"

"Don't you remember, Zelo, when we converted to the Latin alphabet even the elderly people learnt it?"

"The population was only ten million in those days."

"So what? I strongly believe we can do it again. I wouldn't be talking to you without drawing breath like this if I didn't."

"Stop right here and now, you're suffocating me."

"Relax, take a deep breath… Forget everything I've told you so far…"

"How can I do that? You were telling the truth."

"Of course I was, everything I said was true but there's one more truth that precedes everything, everything."

Zelha looks at me quizzically but I continued.

"The girls in the rural areas are waking up, Zelo. Those who are going to school are learning fast. I'm talking of over five thousand girls and that's only the girls being educated thanks to that institution I was talking to you about. And that was only the first, many more have been set up since doing exactly the same thing. Isn't it marvellous, the girls are being educated?"

"And just how do these institutions achieve this?"

"They're helping the families financially to pay for the schooling and the transport. The only condition for receiving the money is that they send the girls to school."

"Are they doing that?"

"As I said, within a period of four years over five thousand girls are going to school."

"Well, well, well, thanks to you Nevo, our country is developing."

"No, no thanks to me, it's thanks to these institutions; they're doing a great job."

"Where do they get the money to do all this?"

"From various sponsors. You know how important support is...whether it's financial or moral."

"Don't I just!"

Zelha knew what that was, of course she knew. I wonder if I could persuade her to start a similar development campaign in her own area.

I took two cigarettes out of the last packet on the table, light them and offer one to Zelha. I wondered if I was mad or something. Have I come here to interview a political prisoner or used this opportunity as an excuse to find my childhood friend, or with a sudden flash of inspiration to persuade her to start another education campaign? Something was telling me that if I could achieve this, it may well be for her own benefit, too. After all, my friend is well known in certain circles for her rebellious nature. It was possible that with such a campaign she may be able to change her image for the better. Who would be able to label a woman who has devoted herself to educating the girls in the East, a rebel? I realised that I was being a bit of a pain in the neck now, for one split second, I recognised that, monotonous tone of a teacher droning away. My father always said that once I had something on my mind, the people around me needed the patience of Job to put up with my ranting and raving on about it. I felt as though, any minute now, Zelha would tip the rubbish on the table, over my head. But still I kept on talking.

"Ignorance seems to have covered the rural areas like a black blanket but once the girls go to school, they have a habit of talking about what they learn to others around them. Believe me, Zelo; this darkness can only be lifted by education, not with money etc... so, in a nutshell, Zelo, all the women in your area need your help."

"I know that, dear. However don't forget I can't do anything from here."

"On the contrary, if you devoted yourself to this whilst you are in here, I'm certain that the girls will sit up and listen."

"OK, OK, I promise," she said in desperation. "If ever I should get out of this place, I promise to look into this matter very seriously but please, Nevo, not another word about it until you're out of here! We've chewed this over long enough now and besides that I have far more pressing problems to attend to than your girls."

"At long last! We seem to have finally made some progress. Your girls have now become my girls."

The topic of conversation continued to focus on the women of the East for a little while longer. We either sent each other up or needled one another while doing so. But, the interesting point was that we were having fun just as we did when we were kids. We always found the funny side of things no matter how serious it was. It was as though that thirty year estrangement never happened. It was as if we had just kissed each other goodnight before going to bed... we had had some peculiar dreams and then suddenly it was morning. I could still see Kader Ana standing at the foot of our beds and telling us to get up. We were awake but we didn't want to get up. We just wanted to lie there chatting. First Zelo had something to say, then me and so, it went on and on.

Time just slipped by without us noticing and here we were again. Two grown ups, two big girls. We've fallen in and out of love, we've been happy and unhappy, married, and had children and jobs. We've done our good deeds and we've sinned... It was as though life itself simply picked us up by the hair, swung us around all over the place before dumping us down on either side of a table in this tiny room; and guess what? We were still talking! Another hour slipped by.

***

We leaned back in our chairs and rested our feet on the empty chairs beside us. Our cigarette ash has formed a little heap on the table. The apple cores have turned brown and we've finished the last packet of biscuits. Zelha noticed me glance at my watch.

"Is our time up?" asked Zelha.

"Yes, what a pity, we've got to part again but please, Zelo, let's not leave it another thirty years before we see each other again."

"Most definitely not, but don't forget I'm banged up in here. God knows when they'll let me out and I can't expect you to come on visiting days, can I?"

"Why not?"

"Well, I know how difficult they make it to get permission, there's so much red tape to cut through. Plus, of course, I would hate it if you got into any sort of trouble because of me. Think of your father, your son and your career. Don't jeopardise any of it on my account. God willing we can meet up when I get out of here, sometime in the future."

"We'll meet very soon, Zelo," I said, trying to hide my sadness. "I believe in this with all my heart and I want you to believe it, too. More and more people realise what's right every day and all the intellectuals of our country are fighting for your freedom."

Zelha smiled a resigned smile.

"Yes, there are a number of people who are very supportive and I'm very grateful to them for it."

Then we remained silent for a while. Obviously neither of us knew what to say next. Zelha broke the silence.

"You didn't get much of your interview done, did you? Will you be able to piece something together from what you've got?"

"It doesn't matter, finding you was much more important. We've managed to carry on from exactly where we left off and rekindled that special friendship. I've managed to put certain things into perspective, I can't tell you how worried I was that you wouldn't remember me. After seeing you the interview became secondary."

"But you've got to write something, haven't you?"

"Yes."

"So what will you write, Nevo?"

"I don't know yet, but I'll think of something. Maybe the best thing to do is to write about our childhood."

"Aren't you going to win our struggle for us?"

"If you're fighting for your identity, freedom and equality, yes, but if you're struggling to save your leader, no."

"We've been talking for hours, Nevo. That man has become the symbol of our struggle, we can't ignore him. As a matter of fact, there are a lot of us who don't like him, me for one and some even think that he is detrimental to the cause but, unfortunately, with his personality he has become the figurehead."

"What a shame."

"What's done is done, Nevo. We must now find a happy medium in order to make any sort of progress. Don't you agree?"

"Isn't a happy medium what I have been suggesting all along? I also agree that both sides need to take a few steps back. But I certainly don't believe in reaching for the impossible… but then that's the way we both are, Turks and Kurds… I think it's a disease of the whole region. It's because of our unrelenting mentality that we're at this point today."

"You may be right but it seems to me that we all share the same mentality, the same attitudes… Neither of us wants to let go of anything… How can we possibly do anything together?"

"Well, we certainly shouldn't give up looking for a solution."

"But we don't agree on the solutions either."

"Yes, now, but I'm sure that we could reach a mutual agreement if only we would sit around the table and discuss things in a civilised manner."

"Haven't we been talking for the past eight hours right here?"

"Come on now, Zelo, we haven't been focusing on solutions alone, have we? We've been catching up on the past thirty years; we've reminisced and even gossiped. And not only about each other but Cengiz, too, and we've certainly put Dede's life under the magnifying glass. That didn't leave much time for focusing on solutions, did it?"

"I suppose not."

"Now, I want you to think very carefully about something you consider extremely important that would help to bring about a solution so that I can write about it in my column."

Zelha thought for a while staring at the ceiling then she looked me straight in the eye and spoke very clearly.

"Yes, here it is. Above all else, the death penalty must be abolished if we are to reach a solution."

"I'll see if I can bring that into my article," I said, trying to hide my disappointment.

"Don't 'bring it in' write about it openly and clearly. That's what my people are expecting."

"I'm interviewing you, Zelo, not your people. Just tell me what you want."

"I just told you."

"Are you suggesting that the future of millions should be jeopardised for the sake of your mad leader? You must be mad, too," I said.

"Would I be in this place if I weren't?"

"My darling, Zelo," I said, trying to imitate the way Dede used to talk to her, "ask me for something that's possible, so that it's at least worth your while, dear girl."

"In that case listen to me very carefully for Dede's sake! Just consider this for a moment. Do you think you could possibly reach an agreement with people whose hero you have hung?"

"You listen to me, too! If a crazy man declares himself a leader and then is the cause of the deaths of thirty thousand people, he should be called a criminal not a hero. The Kurds have rebelled twenty-eight times since the Turkish Republic was founded. If this country of ours has forgiven her rebellious children twenty-eight times, she's bound to forgive them again but don't expect any sympathy for that man."

"Oh! Nevo, Nevo, here you go again trying to get the upper hand. You're only looking at the situation from your own perspective."

"How can you say that? During those five years we were together in Sarıcadam, we often dozed on Dede's lap and he used to stroke our little heads together. I was brought up and nursed by your people. I don't feel any different than you. Have you never read any of my articles? I have written time and time again that our Kurdish citizens should have been taught to read and write their own language, sing their own songs, write their own books and even have their own television channels. Believe me, I have often pointed out that if these mistakes had not been made, we would not have reached the situation we have today. For goodness sake, Zelha, I implore you, tell me which country in the world, be it France, Spain or Italy would tolerate such actions as killing children, extorting money from its people, laying mines in the roads, sucking the life's blood out of them and, as if that is not enough, carrying on with its destructive operations abroad. Tell me, Zelha, who on earth would not react to such atrocities? Who?"

"We keep on going round in circles, Nevo. There's no use arguing like this, you'd better leave now. Write whatever you like. God willing we'll meet again… I'm sure that you and I could never become enemies… but we'd better steer clear of these subjects. You must be able to see it for yourself, we belong to different worlds, we just have to agree to differ."

Suddenly I felt as if I have been stabbed in the heart. I wouldn't let her get away with such a remark if we had plenty of time. I'd love to be able to explain to her that, if the death penalty were abolished and that lunatic in prison was spared, he would still send hundreds of young people to their deaths in search of his impossible dreams. If only I could make her understand that even if one day they should manage to establish their own country, they'll always have to repay the blood money to whomsoever supported them.

They would never be free of the debt they owe to those that backed them up in the first place. If only I could make her see that they are doomed to be puppets with someone else pulling the strings. I wish I could show her examples from both past and present, cases where a country has been founded thanks to the benevolence of a Western power. That new country was doomed never to be free, they would always be answerable to their benefactors. If only I had the time, there was so much I wanted to say to her but, unfortunately, I was expecting Dilaver Bey to be at the door any minute. These problems aside, I didn't want to leave Zelha with resentment in her heart. I crammed the biscuit wrappers, the empty cigarette packets and the apple cores into my bag.

"Haven't you got a plastic bag for that rubbish?" Zelha asked.

"Do you know, Zelha, you'd get on extremely well with my husband? He was a stickler for tidiness just like you."

"I'm glad to hear it. We obviously have things in common since he loved and married you."

"You obviously do! You are both stubborn, fastidious and hard workers."

"The more you tell me about this Murat, the more I think that the two of you should get together again. I rather like him."

"In that case you'd better get yourself out of here as soon as possible, so that I can arrange for you two to meet."

"I'm very happy with the husband I've got, thank you very much. In any case, I could hardly marry my own sister's husband, could I?"

"We may be sisters, yes but… now you're forcing me to say something… isn't it customary in your neck of the woods to offer the widowed brides to their brothers-in-law?"

"You're determined to keep on reminding me of our absurd customs, aren't you? As if your lot do everything right! How about your city ladies who leave their lovely husbands to have affairs with other married men?"

"Don't throw my mistakes back at me or I'll tickle you to death."

"If the cap fits, Nevo, but would you believe me if I told you that I am no longer ticklish. What's more I can no longer laugh or feel happy either."

I got up and walked to her side with wide open arms, "Come here," I said.

Zelha stood up and put her arms around me. I did the same and when I buried my face in her hair, I could smell lemon cologne. I suddenly missed the scent of the earth and grass in her hair of thirty years ago. Could we ever become enemies? Even if we were on opposing sides, armed and in uniform we couldn't hurt one another or our families let alone kill, never! We were like a coin, the two sides are different but we joined together to make one coin.

The door opened and we broke apart.

"Time's up ladies," said Dilaver Bey. "Come along Zeliha Bora, let me escort you to your room and you get yourself ready while waiting for me to return, Nevra Hanım.

Zelha extended her hand to me and looking straight into my eyes said, "I must say, it has been a very fruitful meeting, thank you."

I was holding her hand very tightly and resisted the temptation to press her cold hands to my burning cheeks and simply said, "I can assure you that it was meaningful for me too, thank you."

"Goodbye, have a safe journey."

"Look after yourself, Zeliha Hanım, and remember that there are a lot of people out there thinking and doing their best for you."

We were still holding hands while Dilaver Bey fidgets in the doorway.

"Have you finished your goodbyes?" he asked.

Our hands separated with difficulty and we found it hard to look away from one another, finally she turned her back to me and left the room. I darted to the door which Dilaver Bey wanted to close and held it open. I watch my friend as she was escorted down the corridor. I could see her walking away with her polka-dot ribbon in her hair and carrying my bunny rabbit in its cage.

"Zelha... Zeliha Hanım, Zeliha Hanım..."

Zelha who has walked a few metres away turned and looked at me. She, too, had streams of tears running down her cheeks.

"We'll come up with an effective solution... I promise! We have to... we... we..." My voice echoed back to me along the long stone corridor.

Zelha ran back to me and we hugged each other tightly again in front of a confused Dilaver Bey.

"I'll do my very best... I'll do whatever you want," I whispered in my friend's ear.

"Hush, Nevo, don't cry my love. It's not your fault; it's the fickle finger of fate."

"I'm sure that we can alter the course of this fate… we women… mothers… Please Zelo, don't give up hope. I promise you, I'll write exactly what you want and the message will be loud and clear. You're right, the death penalty solves nothing. It's a primitive option which serves no purpose for anyone, anywhere. No matter what… I promise I will write it… You just wait and see."

Zelha kissed my wet cheeks whispering in my ear, "Don't worry, we are both children of the same earth, we're bound to find a solution. Don't worry!"

"My God!" said Dilaver Bey. "How did this love manage to grow in these few hours?"

Zelha broke away from my arms again but held my hand very tightly one more time before letting go. I shouted after her as she walked away.

"Eze te tu jar ji bir nekim… Bi xatire te." (I'll never forget you, goodbye.)

She turned around and waved goodbye. There was an indescribable expression in her eyes. Love. Endless and unconditional love. Zelha looked at me with that same sparkling smile which came from within just as she did when we were children.

I went back into the room and put on my coat. I took the black shawl from my bag and wrapped it around my shoulders. I sat like a black ghost on the chair waiting for Dilaver Bey's return. There were no thoughts in my head and there was only the Cengiz story on my tape-recorder. There was not a single note written down about the many discussions I had with Zelha. I couldn't even think of what I was to write when I sit in front of my computer. I ought to be concerned, but oddly enough I felt freed, my soul felt like a bird about to take flight.

***

The door opened, "Let's go," said Dilaver Bey.

I picked up my bag and got up. While I was following him down the corridor, he turned to me and said, "Nice to see that you got on so well with Zeliha Bora." He waited for an answer and looked a bit sullen when one was not forthcoming. We continued in single file along the corridor with only the tic-tac sound of our footsteps to be heard. When we were approaching the control point, he reminded me not to forget my mobile phone in a hurt voice. I felt as if I was drunk and my head is spinning, I am in no mood to talk or have a conversation with anyone. In those past few hours I have lived through not just one life but many, in fact, I seemed to have relived a whole slice of history and I was totally exhausted. I did make the effort to say a few kind words to Dilaver Bey before removing the identity badge from my collar and taking back my own identity card and my mobile phone from the security officer. When I got outside into the courtyard, I dialed Hasan Bey's number.

"I'm waiting outside the main gate," he said.

The car was parked outside the high walls and as soon as I got in Hasan Bey asked, "How did it go?"

"Fine, just fine."

He waited for a while for me to continue and then asked, "Just, fine?"

"Yes."

"So, what was she like, what did you discuss, did she tell you anything interesting?"

"She's an amazing woman. We discussed a lot of things... I'm sure you'll be reading all about it."

"I hope nothing went wrong."

"No."

"Dear God! If nothing went wrong why are you so quiet?"

"Sorry, I'm just tired, Hasan Bey, it's been a long day."

"I quite realise that but surely you could just say a few words. You didn't have an argument did you?"

"Why should we argue?"

"OK then, fine. It's just that I felt rather uneasy."

"There was no need I can assure you. After all we're both grown up people."

"Of course you are."

"What's more, unfortunately, we are both capable of seeing the truth."

"And what's that?"

"Both sides are trying to sort out the existing problems with stereotype solutions which don't get results."

"What do you mean by that?"

"Well... for instance... these people have been pushed from pillar to post over and over again. It's about time that we learned that moving people around doesn't serve any purpose at all. What's more, if violence, torture and banning were any good, the problem would have been solved ages ago. It's taken a long time to come to this conclusion but unfortunately there are still some people who insist on sticking to the old methods. This applies to the other side as well. Continuously asking for more, stubbornly asking for the impossible, cutting their noses off to spite their faces and here we are stuck in a state of revolt with them resorting to terrorism... I ask you, what century are we living in? When is this middle-age mentality going to stop? I had long discussions with Zelo, sorry I mean Zelha, for hours. We've gone through the past with a fine- tooth comb. Although we didn't admit it to each other we are both well aware that our people persist in being unrealistic. I must admit this tires me enormously."

"In short then, you have no hope?"

"I wouldn't say that, on the contrary I do have a lot of hope because I strongly believe that, in spite of everything, deep down inside there are still feelings of love and friendship. Even though we speak different languages we've co-existed for centuries so that we share the same feelings and the same emotions. After all, our past is the same, maybe that's why we are so similar which in turn may be why we can neither solve the problems nor sever our ties. But somehow... I believe that very soon we should be able to clear up this sticky situation we've fallen into."

While Hasan Bey was warming up the engine I removed the shawl from my shoulders. I opened the window and leaned out out to wave to Zelo who, as far as I'm concerned, was standing there in the middle of the dusty road wearing her patent leather shoes and her flannel trousers holding on to my rabbit's cage.

"Don't forget!" I shouted, "Don't you dare forget... the solution lies with us, Zelo!"

"Watch it young lady, you'll fall out if you're not careful. It's freezing in here, close the window please," says Hasan Bey.

I was not cold exactly the opposite in fact, I felt all warm inside. My heart was full of love and hope. The longing for a solution lied in my heart like the seeds of the poppies that burst forth in the desert areas of the south-east.

Just as Zelha had said, we are the solution... I know it; I can feel it in my bones. I believe all of us; the Zelhas, the Fatmas, the Sunas, the Berfins, the Leylas and the Emines should listen to our hearts. Both the problem and the solution lie with each and every one of us. After all haven't we all lived and grown up in this land of ours. We have a lot in common; we are quarrelsome, peevish and stubborn but we can also be affectionate, loving and giving. We are sometimes selfish, down right crafty and perfidious and then suffering, innocent and childish. Yes, we are all of these things, children of the same soil.

I draw a large heart in the mist on the window and in the centre form a monogram of the letters T and K standing for Turks and Kurds.

"What's that?" asks Hasan Bey.

"A huge heart," I answer.

"Valentine's day is a long way off yet, isn't it?"

"Maybe, but it will come, won't it?"

"Yes, of course it will, eventually."

Parts of the heart I drew get gradually erased by the car's air-conditioning but somehow the monogram in the centre becomes more pronounced. I interpret this as a good omen. I so very much want it to be a good sign. I lean back in my seat and pray silently.

Please God don't ever separate me from Zelha. May my sister and I never drift apart... you understand me don't you God?.. Please let this wound heal... Maybe it's too much to expect it to happen today, maybe not even tomorrow... but some day... Please... some-day soon."